Protect Me, Cowboy

WILLOW WHITE

NEW CREATION PUBLISHING

PROTECT ME, COWBOY. Copyright © 2023 by Willow White. All rights reserved.

***

This novel is a work of fiction. Names, characters, businesses, organizations, places, events, and incidents are either the products of the author's imagination or used in a fictitious manner.

Chapter 1

The emergency room was slammed. A school bus had gone off the road on its way back from the Air and Space Museum. No one had been seriously injured, but the hospital was full of amped up kids and freaking out parents.

On his way to see his next patient, Dr. Hudson Honeywood was walking quickly so that no one would stop him, and he rounded a corner to see Evelyn Cotton standing in the middle of the hallway. He panicked and jumped sideways to hide—smashing his hip into a metal medical cart. This loud crash was bad enough, but then he saw the stupidly high stack of bedpans wobble. Oh no, it was going to go over. When that pile hit the floor, it was going to sound like a train crashing into a wind chime store. He lunged, swinging his arm to stop it, but only managed to slice the stack in half, so that the pans could spread out and crash into the vinyl floor individually.

He pressed himself against the wall and held his breath as the bedpans banged and clanged, bouncing and rolling in multiple directions. It sounded like a bunch of toddlers let loose with drumsticks and cymbals. Finally, the noise calmed down, and he opened his eyes to survey the damage—and found himself looking into the eyes of his friend Laurel Bannon.

"Are you okay?" The career nurse was concerned, and maybe a little amused.

"Yeah. I'll get them." Hudson straightened his glasses and then tentatively peeked around the corner, hoping Evelyn was gone.

She was, and relief coursed through him as he squatted to collect the bedpans. What was she doing here? She didn't work here. Yet there she had been in all her beautiful glory. And she'd been wearing scrubs and carrying a chart, so she probably wasn't there for a visit.

Laurel scooched to help him. "So what spooked you? Too many kids?"

"No, kids don't usually scare me."

She chuckled. "*Usually*."

"Right." He stood and carried an armload back to the cart. When he turned to get more, Laurel had them all. "Thank you." He helped her arrange them on the cart. "Who left these here? What a hazard."

Laurel snickered. "It wasn't me. I promise." She started to walk away, but she eyed him suspiciously. "Are you sure you're okay?"

He nodded. "I'm sure." He whirled to get back to work and ran smack into Evelyn, whose eyes were bright with mirth.

She glanced behind him at the bedpan cart and then glanced up at him. "I hate it when someone plants a stack of chamber pots in my path."

He laughed. "It wasn't in my path." Why had he said that? Was he about to admit that he'd run into the cart because he'd been hiding from her? And why had he hidden from her? He didn't even know. He was acting like an eighth-grade boy with a crush. "I should have been looking where I was going."

She nodded as if she understood, which she couldn't possibly.

"What are you doing here?" he asked and then wished he hadn't. "Sorry, that sounded ruder than I meant for it to. I mean, do you work here now?"

You have an injured kid to get to, a professional voice in his head scolded.

He'll be fine, the eighth grader argued. *It's just a bruise.*

"I do work here," Evelyn said.

"But why?" He closed his eyes. "Sorry, I guess I took too many of my rude pills this morning."

She laughed, which was charitable of her.

"No worries. And you aren't being rude. Today is my first day."

"Wow. Welcome, then." It didn't make sense. She'd had a better job, a better *paying* job. Why would she come to work at West Hope Hospital?

Dr. Drake was approaching. Oh great, that guy was sure to say something about how Hudson was standing around talking to the pretty nurse. Drake never walked by without saying something snide.

Drake was slowing down. That was even worse.

Hudson braced himself for the gibe.

But Drake didn't deliver one. He did something much worse. He leaned over and kissed Evelyn on the cheek. Then he gave Hudson a dirty look and kept walking.

Hudson was stymied. *What?* The most beautiful woman he'd ever seen was dating *Drake?* What was wrong with her? Drake was the biggest jerk in town, the biggest jerk in medicine, the biggest jerk west of the Mississippi. And Hudson was no expert, but he didn't think Drake was much of a looker either. He looked like Lurch Adams in a lab coat.

Evelyn smiled. "Thad pulled some strings. That's why I'm here." She started to walk off. "It was nice to see you again. I'm glad you didn't let the bedpans win." Still smiling, she gracefully walked away, and he showed great restraint in not watching her go.

Chapter 2

Evelyn Cotton knew quite a few of the West Hope Hospital personnel by sight, but she didn't know any of them well, so she was sitting at a table in the cafeteria all alone, waiting for Thad to join her. But he was late, and her food was growing cold. She knew he'd be annoyed if she started without him, but she was about to do so anyway when Laurel Bannon approached.

"Do you mind if I join you?"

"Please." Evelyn was thrilled. She was comfortable with herself; she was a confident woman; she could sit and eat by herself, but it was still better to have company. And she already felt like people were talking about her. Because she was new. Because she was dating Dr. Drake. It was clear that he wasn't very popular around here. She hadn't yet figured out why.

Maybe she could ask her new friend.

Laurel glanced at Evelyn's food. "They don't use any salt. On anything."

Evelyn laughed. "I noticed, but that's not why I wasn't eating." She picked her sandwich up. "I was waiting for Dr. Drake, but I think he might be standing me up." And then, because she didn't want to talk about whether he was standing her up, she said, "Nice unicorns."

Laurel looked down at her scrubs. "Oh, thanks."

"Do you normally work in pediatrics?" Evelyn couldn't think of another reason the woman would be wearing a thousand tiny unicorns.

"No. So how long have you two been dating?" Laurel took a bite of her pasta.

"A few years." It felt like longer.

"Wow, and you've only just started working here?"

"Yeah. He'd been asking me to move for a while." She forced a chuckle. "I guess he wore me down."

"Move jobs or move in with him?"

"Both, but I only moved jobs. Maybe that's why I gave in to one of his wishes, so I didn't have to do the other."

Laurel raised an eyebrow. "You don't want to move in with him?"

"No, no, I do … it's just that I'm a marriage-before-other-things kind of girl, much to his disappointment." Her cheeks got hot. Had she just overshared? Whoops.

"Oh, of course. That makes perfect sense."

She needed to stop talking about this. It was depressing her. "What about you? Last I knew you worked in home care."

"I did, but things change, and I like it here. Never a dull moment."

"I'll say. Is it always this busy?"

"Almost never. But you know how it is. It's either drought or downpour. Seems like we never land in a happy middle ground."

"I know what you mean. I prefer the droughts, though."

"Oh, me too," Laurel said. "I don't mind being bored."

"Well, I know this is only my second day, but I have a hard time imagining this place could ever be boring." She smiled, thinking of the cute klutz. "I don't think I've ever seen anyone knock over a stack of bedpans, let alone a doctor."

"You saw that, huh?"

"I did. And I felt bad. He seems like a nice guy."

"He is a *very* nice guy," Laurel said. It seemed like she wanted to say more. "Cute too."

The comment surprised her. "Aren't you married?"

"I am, but you're not." Laurel gave her a mischievous smile. "Not yet."

She groaned. "You're not one of those matchmakers, are you?"

"I'm really not. I have no time to even think about anything except my patients and my family." Now that she mentioned it, she was eating rather quickly. Was she even chewing? "But since you brought him up, I thought I'd have some fun."

"Nope, no fun here. I might as well be married."

Laurel scowled. "Marriage *is* fun."

Evelyn laughed. "Then I must be doing it wrong. My first marriage was a complete catastrophe. Thad and I are a much better fit. But I wouldn't call him *fun*." Her words earned her instant guilt. "But I'd take security and comfort over fun any day."

"You know, you can have it all, Evelyn. Security and comfort *and* fun."

Yeah, sure. In the movies, maybe. "Hey, can I ask you an awkward question?"

Looking intrigued, Laurel said yes.

Evelyn leaned a little closer. "It seems like Thad isn't well liked around here. Is that a thing? Or am I imagining it?"

Laurel's obvious surprise embarrassed her. Had that been a stupid question? After some thought, Laurel said, "You know how there's like this friction between doctors and nurses?"

"Yeah," Evelyn said slowly.

"Right. So Dr. Drake is *really* good at that friction. He's hard on the nurses, and so ... we don't go out of our way to interact with him."

"Oh." Well, that was embarrassing since *she* was a nurse. "Thank you for telling me. That's not cool."

Laurel crumpled up the napkin she hadn't yet used and dropped it on her tray. "No problem. And maybe that will get better now that you're here. I had no idea he was dating a nurse. That's one he won't holler at, at least." She chuckled as she stood and grabbed her tray. "Thanks for letting me eat with you. Welcome to WHH. I'm glad you're here."

"Me too," Evelyn said, though she hadn't really decided yet. She watched Laurel walk away. That was one happy nurse. Not that Evelyn was unhappy. But she sure didn't bounce around. And she didn't wear unicorns on her scrubs. What even *was* that?

Finally, Thad walked into the cafeteria. Evelyn straightened, smiled, and waved to get his attention. He smiled at a female doctor before scanning the room for Evelyn. When he saw her, he held up one finger. Then he headed for the pop fountain.

I had no idea he was dating a nurse, Laurel had said. Was that strange? No, she told herself, it was not. Thad hardly knew Laurel. Why should she be kept up to date on his love life? Laurel not knowing about her didn't mean that *no one* knew about her.

Coke in hand, Thad arrived at her table. "Sorry, babe. I ran out of time. I've got to skip lunch today."

"Okay. Do you want to sit for a minute?" She felt guilty. Why did she feel guilty when he was the one standing her up?

"No can do." He bent and kissed her on the top of the head. "But I'll see you tonight, right?"

She didn't answer him, but he walked away anyway.

Chapter 3

"What's eating at you?" Chase asked.

Hudson looked up to see his brother staring at him over the open pizza box. Hudson sighed. If Chase was bringing it up, then that meant Hudson was really acting out of sorts.

"You know that nurse that Dustin keeps giving me grief for?"

It appeared that no, Chase didn't know. But then he said, "Old Mr. Cotton's granddaughter?"

Hudson rubbed his stomach. He never ate pepperoni, and it was already giving him indigestion. "That's the one."

"Oh no," Chase said. "Is she stranded and needs to hide out here at the ranch?"

"Ha ha, very funny."

Chase shrugged. "I call 'em like I see 'em."

"You make it sound like there are damsels in distress lined up at the door."

Chase gave him a stern look. "There used to be a line. You let them all in."

"There were only two of them!" And Olivia and Mindy were no longer in distress. Quite the opposite, actually.

"So what about your nurse?" Chase got up to take care of his plate.

"Do you actually care?"

"I haven't decided yet." He dropped his crusts into the trash bin.

"I appreciate your honesty. Anyway, it's not a big deal, but she's working at the hospital now. I saw her yesterday and again today. She's dating one of the doctors, I guess, and I was just a little lost in thought about how unfortunate that is."

"Sorry, man. Is he a good guy?"

"Not even close." Hudson dropped his pizza on the plate. He had to stop before he did real damage. Comfort food wasn't so comforting if he made himself sick on it.

"Well, then I'm doubly sorry. But what did Mom always say? There's no accounting for taste." Chase headed for the back door.

Grief stabbed Hudson's heart. He missed his parents. He could really use a good talk with his mother right now. She would have something encouraging to say.

It grieved him that she'd gone to heaven with only one of her sons married and without any grandchildren.

And how she would have loved their ranch. She would have been so proud of how good Chase was with the horses. She had always said he had a gift, always said they'd get him a horse of his own as soon as they could afford it. That hadn't happened, and Hudson knew she'd felt guilty about it, which made him feel guilty. She'd been a great mom. And now that she was gone, he wished he had told her that more often. He wished she'd never felt guilty about anything ever.

She would have been such a good grandmother; it wasn't fair. It was only a matter of time now before Wyatt and Olivia had a kid or two. And Hudson knew that Ava was champing at the bit to have kids if Burke would just calm down enough to agree. Soon, babies would be on the way, and Hudson hoped their grandmother could look down from heaven and see them.

And he hoped that someday, she'd be able to see *his* children. He hoped he would get to have children. He still had time, but every day that passed made it feel less likely.

He got up to take care of his plate and the pizza box. There was no use sulking. He had a great family, a great home, and a great career. He needed to stop feeling sorry for himself.

And he needed to stop thinking about Evelyn Cotton. Good men didn't daydream about other men's girlfriends. And Hudson Honeywood cared a great deal about being a good man. He wanted to please God. He wanted to be able to face himself in the mirror. And he wanted to make his mother proud of him.

Chapter 4

Evelyn pulled the lever on the recliner and stretched out. Louis, Thad's basset hound, jumped up onto the couch and settled beside her, lying his heavy head on her thigh. "Let's get some takeout," Evelyn said. "I've been on my feet all day."

Thad didn't look up from his phone. "Aren't you on your feet every day?"

"Yes, but today felt particularly long." The hospital had a much faster pace than her old job, and she hadn't adjusted yet. She enjoyed being kept on her toes, but man, when the hospital was busy, it was stressful.

"You thawed out some chicken."

Only because he'd told her to. "Does that mean you want me to cook the chicken?"

"Well, if we don't, won't it go bad?"

She didn't think so, and she didn't really care if it did. Would the world end if they lost two chicken thighs? This thought made her feel guilty. Fine, she would cook the chicken. In a minute. She closed her eyes and tipped her head back, absentmindedly running her hand over Louis's smooth head and down his back. She'd almost nodded off when Thad said, "Evelyn!"

She jerked alert. "Yeah?"

"Are you hungry?"

"Oh. Yeah." She folded the footrest into the recliner, and then patted Louis on the bum. "Come on, sweetie. Let's go to the kitchen." Louis slid off her and onto the floor and then spread his long tube of a body into an even longer stretch. It looked like it felt good, so she followed his lead. She put her arms up over her head, intertwined her fingers, pointed her palms at the ceiling, and reached up, coming up onto her tiptoes.

Her back cracked like a gunshot. She looked back, expecting a reaction. Thad had to have heard it, but he didn't look up from his phone. *Good thing it wasn't an actual gunshot*, she thought.

Louis followed her to the kitchen and then lay down on the floor to watch her cook, resting his handsome head on his paws. "Sorry, sweetie, it's chicken." If it were beef, she would sneak him a chunk. "You're going to have to wait till it's cooked."

He narrowed his eyes at her, obviously not pleased.

"I know, I know," she muttered. She had to get some sleep. She was feeling cranky, but she hated to leave Thad's place early because she didn't want to leave Louis. Not that anything bad would happen to him after she left. Thad wasn't mean to him or anything. But she didn't like being without Louis. "Wish you could come for another sleepover, honey." She knew he would love that too. They'd done it a few times, once when Thad had gone out of town for a conference and once when he'd traveled out of state for a funeral. Those had been pleasant nights. She wished they could happen more often, but every time she asked Thad about it, it led to him insisting that she move in with him.

He was using the dog as a carrot.

But as much as she loved Louis, she didn't want to move in with Thad. Not only did she think it would be unwise, she also suspected that if she moved in with him, he would never marry her.

Besides, a sleepover with Louis here wouldn't be nearly as much fun as one at her place. Thad didn't even let him in the bedroom, let alone on the bed. When Louis had been at her house, she couldn't even get him to climb onto the bed. At first she'd thought it was because he was chubby, and his legs were stubby. So she'd slid a chair over to the edge of the bed to give him a little step stool. But still, no matter how many times she invited him, patting the bed beside her, he only sat on the floor and looked at her.

Finally, she'd gotten out of bed, scooped him up, and put him on the bed. And then he'd licked her face and wagged his tail for a solid ten minutes before lying down and pressing his body into hers. He'd stayed in that position all night. Evelyn figured that Louis had very much wanted to get on the bed, but he was following the rules he'd been taught.

She felt a little guilty for teaching him to break one of those rules, but only a *little* guilty. Besides, she told herself, when she did marry Thad, she would change his no-dogs-in-the-bedroom rule. It was a cruel and unusual rule anyway.

Evelyn opened a can of baked beans and dumped them into a saucepan. She knew she should make a vegetable too, but she didn't want to have to clean an extra dish. She couldn't believe how tired she was and hoped she hadn't made a mistake switching jobs.

Finally the chicken was done, and she told Thad, who didn't say anything, but he did come out to the table. She set a plate in front of him.

"No vegetable?"

"Beans are a vegetable."

"Beans are a starch." He picked up his fork and dug in.

"A starchy vegetable," she muttered as she got her own plate.

She sat down beside him, cut a small piece of chicken off her serving, and fed it to Louis under the table. Then she ate her supper without really tasting it. She tried to think of something to talk about. She did enjoy talking to Thad. He was smart and witty. But he didn't like talking about work while he ate, and she couldn't think of anything else to discuss.

"Thank you, Evelyn." He pushed his plate away. "That was good." He got up and went back to the couch.

She decided she didn't need to clean her plate and, after giving Louis one more bite of chicken, scraped the rest of it into the trash before doing the dishes. "Sorry, sweetie. If I give you too much, you'll be sorry." This made her wonder if Thad had fed Louis his supper yet. "Did you feed the dog?"

"I thought you did."

Evelyn opened a can of dog food for him and scraped it into his dish. He wagged his tail and then dove in. By the time she had gotten his leash, he was done eating and sat staring at her.

"I'm taking him out." She hooked the leash to his collar and then let him lead her outside. Louis went slowly, more interested in sniffing everything on either side of him than actually walking. Louis saw the whole world through his nose.

Eventually, he spun in seven circles and then did his business. She bagged it up and then pointed them toward home. She walked a little faster now. She was cold and also excited to get home and go to bed, so she had to tug on Louis a bit to keep him from lingering on the exciting scents of dogs who'd come this way a week ago.

When they got back to the house, Thad had turned on the TV and was watching *Dr. Death*. Evelyn shuddered. That was a little weird. She unhooked Louis, threw the baggie in the rubbish bin, and then washed up before going into the living room. "I'm going to head home."

He turned his face to her for a kiss without looking away from the TV.

She gave him a quick peck. "See you tomorrow."

"Okay. Love you."

She glanced at the TV and shook her head. "Love you too."

She found her purse and went to the door. Louis followed her, and she knelt to kiss him goodbye. She ran her hands over his cheeks, pushing back the wrinkled skin. "Good night, handsome. I'll see you tomorrow, okay?" She kissed him between the eyes and then pressed her cheek to his before standing up.

She really hated leaving him. She glanced into the living room and then looked down at Louis. "Get him to marry me, okay?" she whispered. "Then we don't have to do this."

Louis seemed to understand, but he didn't seem to be hopeful.

Chapter 5

Usually Hudson didn't look forward to his hospital shifts, but he was today because he wanted to see a certain nurse. He'd really been working to suppress his attraction, but he wasn't having much success.

Of course, he didn't know if she'd be working, but he had hope.

Laurel caught him scanning the ER and said, "Looking for Evelyn?"

He tried to act innocent. "No. Just grateful things are so calm right now."

"Knock on wood." She laughed and stepped closer. "Can you believe she's dating Dr. Headache?"

He chuckled only because she was laughing. He didn't find it funny. "No, I cannot. I also can't believe you call him that." He tried to look disapproving, but he did take secret pleasure in his colleague's nickname.

"I didn't come up with it." Laurel acted innocent.

"Who did?" Hudson had always assumed it was the nurses, but he didn't know specifically which nurse or nurses had coined Dr. Headache.

"I don't know. I think the nickname has been here as long as he has."

"You should ask Elaine." Elaine was their most senior nurse.

Laurel laughed. "I will. Now you've got me curious." She leaned closer. "And for real, I think you should go for her if you like her."

He groaned. He didn't need that kind of encouragement. "She's taken, and only a jerk goes after another guy's girl."

"True, but ..."

"But what?" How could Laurel, who was a good person, excuse that kind of behavior?

Laurel shrugged. "I don't know. Maybe I'm wrong, but I talked to her briefly, and let's just say that she didn't seem real happy."

"No?" He tried to smash down the optimism that was bubbling up in his chest.

"No. She sounded frustrated that he hadn't proposed yet."

Oh good grief. "That's not unhappy! She wants to *marry* him!" So she loved him, then.

Laurel shushed him. "Here comes Headache now." It was an apt name; Hudson could feel a headache forming.

"You sure are here a lot for a guy with a private practice," Drake sneered.

Hudson was well aware that Drake was jealous of his group practice. "I still have hospital shifts, and right now I'm covering for Dr. Adler."

Drake stared at him for no reason and then looked at Laurel. "You've got a call light on."

Laurel flashed Hudson a small smirk before smiling brightly at Drake. "Sure thing! I'll get right on that!" Her sarcasm was buried beneath good cheer, but it was there.

Hudson waited for Drake to walk away. Why was he just standing there?

Apparently, Drake didn't know either because he finally wandered off in a huff.

What an unpleasant human being. And the most beautiful woman he'd ever seen wanted to marry him. Hudson thought of himself as a fairly smart guy. And he thought he knew a bit about people and how they worked, why they did the things they did.

But maybe he didn't know as much as he thought he did.

As his mother had said, there was no accounting for taste.

Or maybe there was something really wrong with Evelyn. He couldn't imagine what that might be. Maybe she was obnoxious or rude when she wasn't working. Maybe she was a real weirdo who liked to dress up like a clown and set off fireworks near other people's horses. He knew none of this was true, of course, but it made his heart a little less sad to think it.

And then, as if his thinking about her had summoned her, there she was. And wow, was she was breathtaking. She didn't look obnoxious or rude or clownish at all, which was too bad. But he didn't get to admire her for long because as soon as their eyes met, she scurried away as if something had startled her.

Maybe she'd heard fireworks.

Chapter 6

Evelyn's heart skipped a beat when she saw the handsome Dr. Honeywood, so she spent the whole shift avoiding him. She was feeling pretty guilty about how easily he was turning her head. Of course, she'd had a soft spot for him ever since he'd been so good to her grandfather. He had shown real patience and compassion and gone out of his way to help her grandfather save face. Dr. Honeywood was a good doctor. No wonder he had a successful group practice. His patients probably loved him. She knew how much Thad wanted to have a small practice. He talked about it quite a bit, but he thought he would have to move, that the population in the area wouldn't support another small office. And he didn't want to move, which was a good thing because she didn't either. She'd lived her whole life in the area. She had roots here. Family. Friends. She was glad he didn't want to move.

Evelyn heard Thad's voice and looked up. He was scolding Laurel for something. Evelyn didn't know what, but he was being really loud. She was embarrassed for both of them. And though she didn't think she had any business getting involved, her feet carried her in that direction anyway. She was thankful that it was over before she got there. Laurel, to her credit, seemed unfazed.

Thad did not.

"Is everything okay?" Evelyn asked.

"Yes, I'm fine," he snapped. "This has nothing to do with you!" He stalked off.

Whoa. His voice had gotten louder with each word, and she did not appreciate that. She looked around, hoping no one had seen the scuffle, and far too many people had. She put her head down and got back to work, but when he joined her in the cafeteria, she lit right into him. "I don't appreciate you hollering at me in front of my coworkers. They don't even know me yet, and then you embarrass me like that." Her blood was boiling. She was even angrier than she thought.

"I didn't holler at you." His tone dismissed her. "Stop being so dramatic."

Somehow, her anger got hotter. Yes, he was a doctor, but she knew her strengths, and she knew he wasn't better than her or smarter than her. He certainly wasn't kinder than her. "You know that doctors aren't supposed to holler at nurses, right? Regardless of whether they're dating them. I wouldn't put up with that from any doctor. Our relationship doesn't mean I'm going to give you a pass."

He rolled his eyes. "She deserved it. She was fifteen minutes late with a—"

When had they shifted from talking about her to talking about Laurel? Oh well, close enough. "I don't care *what* she did." Evelyn leaned across the table. The cafeteria was crowded, and she didn't want to be overhead. And Thad was being really loud. "She's a nurse, she's a professional, and you don't holler at coworkers in public. Good grief, what is wrong with you?" Maybe she shouldn't have come to work with him. She didn't like knowing him in this setting.

"I don't even know why she's here."

"What? What does that mean?"

"It means that she married a stinkin' billionaire. Would you go to work if you married a billionaire?"

No, probably not. But she'd never know because she was marrying this dolt. "Maybe she enjoys her work."

"No one enjoys their work that much."

It was Evelyn's chance to roll her eyes, and she took it. "So then what's your theory? What other reason could she possibly have to be here?"

He shrugged. "Mental illness?"

"Wow." She dropped her spoon and just stared at him.

"What?"

"I don't like seeing you like this. Maybe I shouldn't have come to work with you."

"It's not too late to leave."

He might not have meant those words to be hurtful. She didn't think he had. But wow, did they hurt. He had *begged* her to come work at this hospital. She'd given up a job she loved. She had walked away from *patients* she loved.

For this? "It *is* too late, Thad." Her voice was choked with tears, which she hated. "I quit my job, remember?"

"I'm sure they'd take you back." Again with the dismissive tone.

And no, they probably wouldn't. They'd already replaced her. "Is that what you want?" What was happening here? She'd worked so hard to make him happy, but he seemed so unhappy.

"No, I want you here with me but not if you're going to undermine me and criticize the way I do my job."

"I wasn't criticizing the way you ... you know what, never mind." She sighed. It was like trying to reason with a mule. "And I don't think the Bannons are literal billionaires. I think people just say that. For all we know all their money is tied up in land and cattle. They might not even have any cash for—"

"No, they're *filthy* rich. It's old money from the gold rush days. It's not like they earned it."

Wow, he was one jealous man, wasn't he? She gathered up her things. "I've got to get back to work, but you do know that the Bannons give away thousands and thousands of dollars to all sorts of causes, right? Doesn't sound too filthy to me."

"Thousands is a drop in the bucket when you've got billions."

"Whatever." She had endured enough. She stood up and started to walk away but then stopped and looked down at him. "But I'm serious, Doctor"—she kept her voice low, but he could hear her—"do not holler at me or any other nurse in front of me again, or I'll be going to HR." She knew that he thought she was bluffing, but she didn't care. If he gave her a chance to make good on that promise, she would do just that. She didn't want to get him in trouble, but being in love with him didn't mean she was willing to sacrifice her professional dignity for him.

And she didn't think she should have to.

Chapter 7

Hudson blinked his eyes open and was super happy to realize it was a Saturday. He'd fulfilled his hospital commitment for the month, and now he could work on forgetting about Evelyn Cotton.

He was never going to admit it to his brothers, but he had even downloaded a dating app. He hadn't connected with anyone yet, but he was seriously considering sending a message to a hair stylist in Rapid City. She wasn't as pretty as Evelyn, but she was very attractive, she liked horses, and he needed a haircut.

But before any of that could transpire, he had to go grocery shopping, a chore he hated doing, but he couldn't let Chase do it or they'd be eating nothing but steaks and pickle-flavored potato chips for the next week.

The grocery store was packed, and Hudson wondered if the locals were there to take advantage of the store's stellar air conditioning. Western South Dakota was in the middle of an autumn heat wave, and it was hotter than the blazes out. Chase had reminded him three times to get ice cream sandwiches. It was very important to him to get the mint chocolate chip ones. Every once in a while Chase acted like he was fourteen again. Hudson was happy to encourage that. Chase had been a happy teenager.

Hudson grabbed his cart and started dropping items into it, motivated to get to the checkout line before it grew any longer. He was about to pick up Chase's cheese crackers when he saw her.

Evelyn.

To avoid smashing into an unseen stack of loud metal objects, he looked to his right to make sure his escape was clear and then slowly ducked out of sight. Then he froze. Now what? He still needed the Cheez-Its.

He discreetly looked up at the mirror on the ceiling. Was Dr. Headache with her? His chest relaxed. It seemed she was alone. Good for her, busting out for some freedom.

Hudson slunk around the corner to continue his shopping. Chase could live without his extra bold ridged crackers this week. Glancing up in the mirrors every few minutes, Hudson succeeded in giving Evelyn a wide berth. It wasn't that he was afraid of her, but he'd done a decent job of putting those pesky feelings of his to bed. He didn't want to wake them up.

So yeah, maybe he was a little afraid of her.

He was reading the ingredients on a can of organic soup when he caught some movement in his peripheral vision. He looked up to see people running toward the back of the store. Not walking quickly. Actually running.

Assuming the store was being robbed by armed villains, he looked up at the mirror and saw that *everyone* was running toward the back. There was no gunman near the measly two registers—there was no one near the registers at all. Even the clerk was heading for the back wall.

And then Hudson knew what was happening. He searched the mirror for Evelyn, found her, and headed her way. She had fallen in with the stampede, and he cut into it to grab her arm. Now he could hear the winds outside. "There's no room in there!" he hollered.

He pulled her toward the side of the building, toward the walk-in cooler. She went with him willingly enough, and they picked up speed. As they ran, the front windows exploded—the glass shards hitting the floor sounded oddly peaceful, an unfitting soundtrack as the wind grew louder. Merchandise and shelves started to topple as the wind ripped through the holes it had created.

Behind them, ten different phones went off with emergency alerts. *Great timing*, he thought as he pulled her into the back room and then toward the walk-in cooler. The walls creaked; the floor beneath their feet vibrated with a current that felt electric.

Four steps to go. Five at the most.

It felt like the building exploded. His ears popped, and he felt the floor lift beneath him as he yanked Evelyn into the cooler. She said something, but he couldn't hear her. All he could hear was metal creaking and tearing like a chorus of wailing banshees.

He let go of Evelyn for a second to use both hands to shove a giant crate of melons into the doorway. He didn't want to get trapped in the cooler. And then the cooler was shaking, and he hooked his arm around her waist and pulled her down to the floor before covering her body with his. He took care not to squish her and to protect her head and face, and then he held on.

God, spare us. Spare us all. Make it pass over us.

After one final sickening tearing sound, a terrible cry sounded from the opposite side of the cooler, and Hudson braced himself for the weight of a building to fall on his back.

But nothing touched him, and then everything went eerily quiet.

The lights blinked once and then went out, which made things feel even quieter.

He'd never been exposed to such a quiet. It was powerful and terrifying.

And it was soon interrupted when the cooler's compressor kicked on. Well good, at least they would be cold while they waited for rescue. He stayed put for another few seconds to be sure it was over before lifting himself off of Evelyn. He looked down at her face, which was wet with tears. "Are you okay?" His voice was croaky.

Keeping her eyes squeezed shut, she gave him an almost imperceptible nod. Holding her breath, she didn't move except to bring one hand up to wipe away the tears.

"Hey," he said softly, and then he couldn't help but assist her with wiping away those tears. He barely touched her. Just enough to transfer the tears from her skin to his. "Hey, we're okay. Take a breath."

Her lips curved into a smile—barely—and she inhaled deeply and then exhaled slowly. Good. She could breathe. That was a bonus.

He turned to survey the damage. His strategically placed crate of melons had been crushed to a fraction of its width—spraying honeydew juice in all directions. It dripped, forming small, sweet puddles on the cooler's floor. But the crate had held the door open, which was a good thing because the emergency lighting spilling through that crack was their only source of light. If he hadn't moved the melons, they would be in pitch black right now, and he didn't have his phone.

The cooler was situated against the outside wall of the building. He'd chosen to hunker down beside the inside of the cooler, and that wall stood tall and straight. The outside wall—not so much. It now stood at a forty-five-degree angle to the floor. He studied the top of it, trying to sense movement, but he couldn't see any. He didn't know how much weight was pushing down on that cooler wall—or the outside wall of the building for that matter—but for now, it was holding.

He looked down at Evelyn. "Are you okay for a second? I'm going to take a look." He realized then that his hand was still resting lightly on her arm, and he self-consciously removed it.

She sniffled. "I'm not an invalid. You can get up."

He chuckled. "Okay." He got up on legs that he wished were less shaky. That surge of adrenaline had left him a little wobbly.

Careful not to step in the sticky melon puddles, he leaned over the squashed crate to push the cooler door open—and it didn't budge.

Oh boy.

The crate had kept the door from closing completely, but it hadn't held it open enough to let them out. Evelyn wasn't a large woman, but even she wouldn't be able to slide through an eight-inch gap.

He lowered his shoulder and leaned into the door with all his might, taking care not to grunt in front of the pretty woman, but it was like pushing against a cement wall. And maybe that's exactly what he was doing. There was a good chance a cement wall had caved in on this cooler door. He stood up. Maybe he should stop pushing, then. He didn't want any weight to shift anywhere.

He straightened to return to Evelyn, who was staring at his boots. He looked down to see that he'd stepped in the juice puddle. Fantastic. His favorite boots had become ant traps.

"Are we stuck?" she asked, her voice impressing him with its strength.

"For now, yes." He studied her. Was she uncomfortable being trapped in this small space with a man she hardly knew? She didn't seem to be. Something was wrong, though. "Are you in pain?"

She shook her head quickly. "I'm good."

"Okay, good." She wasn't good, though. That was obvious.

He traveled the small perimeter of the cooler, looking for any signs of peril, but he didn't see any. It seemed they were safe for now. It looked like the cooler had done all the collapsing it was going to do.

He returned to Evelyn, who had sat up and leaned against the bottom shelf that ran along the cooler's wall. She was watching him, and for the first time, he felt self-conscious about plucking her out of the crowd and dragging her in the opposite direction. All so she could have the honor of being trapped in this small space with him.

Was he a hero or a kidnapper? "Sorry," he said without thinking.

She scowled through her tears, which still flowed freely. "What for?"

He didn't know how to answer that. He didn't want to sound like he'd regretted his split-second decision. He didn't know yet if he regretted it. He didn't know yet how the others had fared. "I've been in that bathroom," he said. "It's not big. I didn't know if all those people were going to fit."

"Oh. Is that where they were going? I figured there was a shelter in the back of the store or something."

"There is. Sort of. The bathroom is marked as a tornado shelter, but it's too small. Granted, when they built it, West Hope wasn't quite the metropolis it is now." It had been an attempt at humor, and it had been ill-timed.

Her eyes grew wide. "So all those people ... do you think they are okay?" She started to get up. "We have to get to them. They might need medical attention." She winced as she put weight on her right foot and crumpled back to the ground.

"You're not okay," he said, going to her.

She held him off with a hand. "I'm fine, I'm fine." She tried to get up again, using the wall for support.

"We can't get out. I can't push the door open."

"I'll help you."

He didn't think she was a weakling, but he didn't think she was strong enough to make a difference against that door either. "I don't want to push too hard. We don't know what's on the other side of that door. I don't want anything to shift."

"Oh." She slid back down to the floor.

"There's a very good chance they all made it and are packed in there safely," he said. He hoped.

"It would be awful to be trapped in there with that many people."

"Maybe they're not even trapped. Maybe they have all walked out of the store by now. Maybe they're climbing into their trucks and driving away."

She gave him a sardonic look. "We haven't heard a peep."

He nodded toward the compressor. "Hard to hear anything over that hum, and we're quite a ways from the bathroom. A lot of different scenarios could be playing out without us hearing about it." He did, however, think they were close enough to hear wails of anguish, and he hadn't heard any, so that was a good sign. And he was certain that help was on the way. "Do you have your phone?"

"Yeah." She reached to her right, and then froze. "No. It's in my cart." She looked up at him, and her beauty nearly took his breath away. He realized he was towering over her and that this was weird, so he sat down beside her. "I'm so sorry," she said.

"No need to be sorry. It's not like I said, 'Hey, grab your phone and we'll go hang out in the walk-in cooler!'"

She chuckled, but it sounded mournful.

"And I'm sorry too. Your phone made it further than mine did. Mine is still in the truck."

"Did you hear all those tornado warnings going off on their phones? I would have laughed if I hadn't been so terrified."

"I did," he said. "I want to say better late than never, but I'm not sure that applies here." For the first time, he noticed how swollen her right ankle was. "Whoa, no wonder that hurts." He felt guilty for not noticing before. He should have looked her over, especially once he suspected she was injured. He scooted down to get a closer look, and she winced when he pressed his fingers to her skin.

"I'm okay. It's not broken."

"No? Are you superman?"

She scowled. "What?"

"Do you have x-ray eyes?" He grinned. He was trying to be funny, and he was failing.

"No, but I have a sense about these things."

He believed her. "May I?"

She nodded and held her breath. He did a quick examination, not learning any more than he already knew. He looked around the room for something cold, but there wasn't much to offer her. He doubted that she wanted to press a hunk of wet honeydew to her ankle. Or a carrot. Maybe he should have dragged them into the freezer. Then they'd have frozen peas, at least.

"It's okay, really." But her continuous tears suggested she was still in pain.

Maybe too much. He knew how bad a sprained ankle could hurt, but it seemed her pain was disproportionate to her injury. "Are you hurt anywhere else?"

She shook her head. "I'm good."

Maybe she had a low tolerance of pain. He needed to distract her. "First tornado?" He tried to make his voice light. Levity was a good thing.

"Yeah."

He slid back against the wall. "Mine too. But I think we did okay for first timers. We're alive. No serious injuries. Help is on the way."

"Not to be impatient, but I'm surprised I haven't heard sirens yet. We're less than a mile from the fire department."

"Sometimes it takes a minute if more than one building got hit."

"Oh, of course. Duh. I didn't think of that. Sorry, didn't mean to be selfish."

He longed to touch her, to put his arm around her. He didn't. "It has never occurred to me that you are selfish. And they'll get to us eventually. Besides ..." His eyes returned to the carrots. "... at least we won't starve to death."

A fresh sob exploded out of her.

"Hey, hey." He laid a hand on her leg. "It's okay. We're okay."

"It's not us I'm worried about."

"Oh." Was she thinking about the people in the bathroom? "I'm sure everyone else is fine too. I shouldn't have said what I said about the bathroom. I didn't mean to scare you."

"No, it's not that. I mean, of course I'm worried about them too, but ..." She let out another small wail.

When she didn't continue, he said, "What is it?"

"You'll think it's stupid ..."

"I bet that I don't." No matter what it was, he would be sure to not act like it was stupid.

She took a shaky breath. "My dog is in my car." Fear shook her voice. "Or he was, anyway."

Empathy rushed through him. "Oh, okay, I get it." He gave in and put his arm around her, pulling her into him. "Listen, you probably already know this, but let me remind you that tornadoes are weird. They follow a path, leaving objects to the left or the right of that path untouched. Your dog is probably absolutely fine." He worked to believe this was true. He didn't want her to hear doubt in his voice, and he also really wanted it to be the case. He almost asked her where she had parked, but if she had parked right out front, he didn't know if he would be able to hide his disappointment.

She answered his unspoken question anyway. Maybe she'd heard him think it. It wouldn't be the first time a nurse had read his mind. "I parked way off to the side so that he could have some shade if the sun came out. I left the car running, so he might not have even needed the shade ..." She sighed. "I probably shouldn't have brought him, but I was only planning to be in here for a minute, and I just really, really wanted to bring him." She sounded so guilty, and he hated it. "Oh, Louis, I am so, so sorry."

"Please, I'm begging you. Let yourself believe that he's perfectly fine and that he's patiently waiting for you to get out of here."

She took a shaky breath. "I'll try."

Chapter 8

Chase drove into the grocery store's parking lot too fast and had to slam on the brakes to keep from running into a car that sat crooked in the entrance. It's windshield had been smashed, presumably by the shopping cart that still sat askew on its dented hood. In his head he heard Hudson complaining about people who didn't return their carts, was annoyed by this, then felt guilty for being annoyed, and prayed aloud that Hudson would still be around to annoy him further.

His truck idling, he looked at the wreckage before him. His head swam, and he tightened his grip on the steering wheel to ground himself. He took a deep breath. *You are in West Hope, South Dakota. You are home. You are home. I am home. I am home.* He exhaled purposefully.

He had never seen the aftermath of a tornado in the Middle East, but he'd driven up on scenes eerily similar to this one. And that similarity was wreaking havoc on his mind, as well as his stomach.

But he couldn't drive away. There were people in there, and from the looks of it, a lot of them. Why on earth had there been so many people here at once? What terrible timing. He eased his truck around the cart-car and looked for Hudson's truck.

He found it in a pile of vehicles up against a large concrete base for a light pole. The light pole was gone. Shaking his head, he took another deep breath, prayed again for strength, sanity, and help, and then turned off his engine and got out of the truck. Somewhere nearby, a dog barked, but that was the only sound. He didn't hear humans calling for help, and this gave him a very bad feeling. *Think. Don't feel. Think.* Okay, there were a bunch of people in the store. Someone had to have seen the tornado coming, and that person would have warned them, and then they all would have run to the tornado shelter, right? Which was the bath—*oh no.*

Way too many cars. Tiny bathroom.

The small shelter was in the back of the building, and he headed that way. With every step closer to the building, his dismay grew. This was some serious damage. Most of the front of the store stood tall, like a false wall in a fake wild west town. This front wall offered hope that the rest of the scene knocked down. The left third of the building was completely gone, and Chase prayed that no one had been in it. Most of the roof had been ripped off, some of the walls had caved in, and unbelievably, a delivery truck was upside down on the right far wall. Chase guessed that it had landed on the roof and then slid off onto the ground before the roof completely collapsed beneath it. He added an addendum to his prayer: *Don't let anyone be under that truck.*

When he rounded the back left corner of the building, his heart leapt when he heard voices. "Hello?" he cried out, and then a chorus of voices rose from the rubble to answer him. And even though they were far away, and in desperate need of help, the sheer number of them caused him fear, and that fear brought him shame. *God, make me keep it together.* "It's Chase Honeywood!" he called out. "Is everyone okay?"

Too many people tried to answer, but he got the gist of it: it was very crowded, but everyone was alive. "Is my brother in there?" He hadn't heard his voice, but that didn't scare him yet. Hudson wouldn't be one of the ones trying to outscream the others, and if he was in there, he was busy helping anyone who was scared or hurt.

But he wasn't in there. One of the female voices hollered at everyone else to shut their mouths, and then, when a hush fell, she called out, "Hey, Chase! It's Deedee. I saw Hudson in the store, but he's not in here. I saw him going toward the deli." Chase's eyes leapt to the other side of the building. *Oh no.* "I'm guessing he was heading for the walk-in. He had a woman with him."

A woman? What woman? Had he secretly met some woman at the grocery store?

Chase thanked Deedee, and she explained that none of their phones worked.

He glanced in the direction of the only nearby cell tower, which had to be overloaded, *if* it was even still standing. "The firemen are at the Pizza Ranch. A bunch of kids got trapped, but I'm sure help will be here soon." As he talked, he looked for a way to get to them. Maybe he could help them himself. But he would have to dig, and there was a *lot* to dig. "I'm not leaving!" he called out. "Holler if you need something."

He hurried around the back of the building and heard the dog barking again. He followed the sound to the vehicle it was coming from, a small car that had been blown onto its side. The driver's side window pointed at the sky. The windshield was cracked, but still intact, and a frantic basset hound was pawing at it maniacally.

Poor thing. "Hang on, buddy. Let me see if I can get you out of there." Chase climbed up onto the side of the car, hoping that the door had been left unlocked, and if it had, that he could get it open even though it was now parallel with the ground.

It took some elbow grease, but he was able to pull it open.

The dog shot out of the car like a jack-in-the-box, its ears flying out to either side to make it look especially acrobatic. Chase grabbed it out of the air with one arm and brought it to his chest as he lowered the car door shut with his other arm. The dog wiggled wildly to get free.

"Hang on, hang on. Let me get you to the ground." Chase jumped off the car and then set the dog down. He took off like a shot toward the store, barking his head off. When he reached the delivery truck, he slammed on the brakes and started baying at the cement wall in front of him.

Wow, good job, boy.

Chapter 9

Evelyn had never been so scared, but she was doing her best to hide it. She tried to tell herself that Louis was just a dog, that there were people in danger—actual human souls—but she remained terrified for him. Yes, he was just a dog, but he was also her best friend. He was her family. And she was so scared that he'd been scared—or was still scared. Scared that he'd been hurt and was suffering, and she couldn't get to him to comfort him. A new sob escaped her, and she put her head in her hands, embarrassed.

"It's okay." Hudson pulled her in tighter. She'd barely registered when he'd put his arm around her. It had felt so natural. Probably just the circumstances. She resisted the urge to nuzzle further into him. She wanted to. She wanted that comfort and warmth, but she didn't want to be inappropriate. She had a boyfriend.

The compressor quit running, which brought an unexpected relief. "Wow, I didn't think that was very loud until it quit. That's nice."

"Yeah." He looked uneasy.

"What is it?"

He tried to shrug it off. "Nothing, really. I normally like quiet, but this is almost too quiet." He shook his head. "It won't last, though. The cold will leak out through the door, and it will kick back on." He leaned back and then immediately straightened. "Hey," he whispered, "did you hear that?"

She held her breath and concentrated. "What did you hear?" she asked after a moment.

"I'm not sure," he said, but she could tell he had a theory.

"What do you *think* you heard?"

He didn't answer her, but he was obviously still straining to hear whatever it was. Voices? Sirens? More wind? "Was it a good sound or a bad sound?"

He still didn't answer her, and she was starting to get annoyed, but then she heard it.

Barking.

"Louis?" she cried out, getting to her feet as quickly as she could. Then she held still and listened, keeping all her weight on one foot.

Hudson came to a stand beside her.

"Could you tell which direction it came from?" she asked.

"Not really, but I'm assuming outside."

She looked at him. "Was that a joke?"

"Sorry. Just trying to lighten the mood."

She hobbled to the crooked wall and then held still, and she heard it again. It was so faint she might have been able to convince herself it wasn't real, but Hudson had heard it too. "He's alive." The two words rode her exhale and were barely audible.

"Yes, he's alive." Hudson sounded like he believed her, but she was still self-conscious.

"I know all dogs sound alike, but I'm telling you, that's him."

"I know. I'm sure you can tell."

"Louis!" she yelled out. "You stay right there! I'll be right out!" She closed her eyes, embarrassed. Louis probably couldn't understand her, but she'd had to say something. She listened carefully, but there was no response. Her ankle was killing her, so she sat back down, though she couldn't lean on the slanted wall.

Hudson didn't join her, and she looked up to see him looking nervous. He didn't trust that wall to hold. She scooted back to their original wall, and then he sat beside her again. He didn't put his arm around her this time, and she missed it. After a quiet minute, he asked, "How long have you had Louis?"

"Oh, he's not my dog," she said quickly.

The look on Hudson's face brought out a laugh that shot pain through her ankle. As a nurse, she knew that everything in her body was connected, but this was better proof than she'd ever had. *Note to self: don't laugh so suddenly when you have a sprain.* "Okay, so he's my dog *emotionally*. And the dog would agree with that. I've known him about two years, but technically, he is Thad's dog."

Understanding registered on Hudson's face before she finished her explanation, and his disappointment was evident. For some reason, this made her talk more. "Thad got Louis when he was ten weeks old, and Louis was two when I met him. So even though he's not my dog, I've been his best friend for half his life. I'm the one who loves him, and I am clearly his favorite." She forced a chuckle, and it sounded every bit as fake as it was.

"Hard to believe that the dog would choose you over Dr. Drake."

It took her a second to realize that he was being ironic. "Oh, yeah. Well, Thad's not real affectionate."

"And yet you want to marry him."

She couldn't tell if that had been a question. "Who told you that?" As soon as she'd asked the question, she knew the answer. "Laurel."

"Sorry, don't be mad at her. Laurel and I have known each other a long time. She didn't say much, only that you mentioned that you were planning to marry him. Forgive me for being completely mystified by that." He was staring at her, and his gaze was making her warm all over, which was significant as their little hidey-hole was pretty cold.

"He's different outside of the hospital." She realized too late that she was mumbling. Why had she mumbled that? "He is," she insisted.

"I would certainly hope so."

She stared at him. She couldn't believe that the hyper-polite, mild-mannered Hudson Honeywood could be such a little snot. "Yeah. He is."

In the distance Louis barked again. And then again.

"I wonder if someone is out there," she said. "Maybe he's trying to tell them that we're here."

"Maybe. If so, I doubt they need him to tell them. There were a lot of people in the store."

"Yeah, but we don't know whether or not they're out. Maybe we're the only ones left."

"Don't worry." He softened his voice. "They know we're in here."

"How?" She wasn't really worried about spending the rest of her life in the refrigerator, but she wondered how he was so confident.

"It's a small town. People take attendance without even realizing they're doing it. They know who's missing."

"And your truck is out there, with Honeywood Ranch emblazoned on the side."

"I don't know if it's emblazoned, but yeah." He sounded defensive. "I wonder how Louis got out of your car."

Had he just changed the subject? "I don't know." She tried to think of an explanation that would leave Louis unscathed. "Maybe the wind broke a window."

"Maybe. Well, at least we know that he's okay. That was nice of him to let you know. I can't believe Drake named his dog Louis."

She snickered. "Why's that?"

"I don't know. Just doesn't seem pretentious enough."

"Wow, you are so right." She didn't want to admit that, but Hudson had been so on the nose, he deserved some credit.

"Yeah? How so?"

"Technically, the dog's name is Pasteur. That's what it says on his papers, but that was so entirely ridiculous that I started calling him Louis. And it suits him."

Hudson was laughing and obviously trying not to. He pinched the bridge of his nose. "Pasteur. That's just so ... what's the word I'm looking for ..."

"Pretentious?" she offered.

"No, that's not quite it. Oh, I know! *Gross*."

She wanted to laugh, but she held it in. "It's nice to hear a doctor agree with that. I thought maybe I was missing the genius of it because I'm just a lowly nurse."

"You are not lowly. No nurses are. Doctors could never do what they do without nurses."

"It's good to hear you say that too."

An awkward pause filled the air between them. It was thick with a tension she didn't know how to relieve.

"So the dog just started answering to a new name?" Hudson blurted out.

"I don't think he ever actually answered to Pasteur. But I'm also not sure Thad used it much. I'm not sure he paid Louis much mind at all."

"Why did he ever get a dog? He doesn't seem the type."

"He said that he was after a veterinarian, and so he needed a puppy."

Hudson groaned. "Just when I thought the story had reached maximum grossness."

Evelyn laughed and then felt guilty. This was her man they were poking fun at. "He does have strong points, I promise. But his dog parenting isn't one of them."

"Please, tell me. What are his strengths?"

She took a big breath, trying to decide where to start. "Uh ... he's a great doctor. He is crazy smart. He's witty and charming and ... and he makes me happy."

"Good. You deserve to be happy, Evelyn. And I mean that. Hey, how's your grandfather doing?"

Another abrupt subject change. Hudson was good at those, apparently. "He's doing great. We got him into Sunny Acres, and they are taking great care of him."

"That's good to hear. And he wasn't upset about moving there?"

"He was at first. My mom wanted to let him live with her, and he wanted that too, but we couldn't make it work. He kept wanting to leave her house on his own. He didn't understand that he couldn't just jump in the truck and go for a drive anymore, and it's not like she could wrestle him back into the house and tie him to a chair until his urge to wander passed. And one of the last times he did get away from her, he went to the Dairy Queen and then forgot who he was and where he lived. Scared us half to death."

"That is scary," he said, and she was impressed with his sincerity. "I like Doug. I have always liked Doug. He is good people."

She appreciated that he kept the compliment in the present tense. So many people talked about what a great man her grandfather used to be, which drove her nuts. He was still a great man. He wasn't dead yet. "I hope he's okay right now," she said. "I can't believe there was a stupid tornado. I never saw any tornado watch or warning or anything."

"Me neither, which might well mean that it was the only one."

"And they can just appear out of nowhere like that? I mean, I've lived in South Dakota my whole life, and I can't remember that happening before."

"I remember it happening once when I first started working at the hospital before I had my own practice. It didn't hit us, but it gave us quite a scare."

"Speaking of which, aren't you kind of young for a private practice?"

"I don't think so, but I wouldn't have been able to do it without my partner."

"Well, Thad is some jealous of you." Whoops, maybe she shouldn't have said that.

"Did he say that?"

"Not directly, but yeah. He finds it pretty annoying that you've managed to start your own business, and he hasn't." Had she just sounded like a jerk? She wasn't sure. "Sorry, I didn't mean to make it sound like it was easy. I know that you worked for it." He didn't say anything. "What made you decide to do that?" She thought she knew the answer to this—more freedom, more money—but she wanted to keep the conversation going.

"I really like working with families. I like getting to know a family and helping them with lots of different things. I wanted people to know their doctor, know they could count on me. I mean, there's nothing wrong with the urgent care model, necessarily. It has its place in the world. But I've always found the small-town doctor who knows you by name kind of a romantic concept."

Despite the throbbing pain in her ankle, the idea was soothing. "That certainly is a throwback to simpler times."

"Yep. To a time when people really knew each other. For better or for worse."

She laughed lightly. "Exactly. Sometimes it's not awesome to know everything about someone."

"No, but even then there is some comfort in it. I think we're supposed to know one another even when stuff is hard. I don't think we're supposed to do life alone."

At his words a pang of loneliness stabbed at her heart, which didn't make sense. She wasn't lonely, and she wasn't alone. She wanted to keep talking, but maybe they could discuss something a little less ... real. She didn't want to be contemplating whether she was lonely. Not while she was trapped in a cold box with a warm doctor she *wasn't* dating.

Her eyes landed on the door. "I'm so glad you propped that open. Even if we can't get out, it makes me feel less claustrophobic. I can't believe you had the presence of mind to do that."

"Not sure about presence of mind. I just didn't want to be trapped."

"That's fair."

"Are you claustrophobic?" he asked.

"Not usually, but I've never been trapped in a refrigerator during a tornado either."

He laughed. "You're funny. I didn't realize you were so funny."

This caught her by surprise. No one ever thought she was funny. "Can I ask you a question? And I swear I'm not flirting."

He chuckled. "Who could turn down a question after an intro like that?"

She wasn't sure what to make of his statement. Had she offended him? "I was just wondering how on earth you are still single."

"Oh, that's easy."

"It is?"

"Yeah. I've just never gotten married."

She laughed. "Smart butt. You know what I mean."

"I do. So my mother always drilled into us boys that we shouldn't hurry to get married, that we should wait till we knew for sure. She would say, 'God already has a wife picked out for you. Don't be in such a hurry that you're hitched to the wrong horse when the right one shows up.'"

Smart woman. Evelyn had married the wrong man. She knew the damage it could do. "Somehow that's both practical and romantic."

"I don't know if anyone ever accused my mom of being a romantic, but she sure was practical. She had a lot of wisdom. But as for me, I guess I've just been waiting till I knew for sure. But to be honest, I've never even come close. I've dated, but I've never met anyone I would want to grow old with. I mean, people are annoying. I don't want to accidentally commit the rest of my life to someone who will only get more annoying with age." He laughed.

She laughed with him but then stopped short when she imagined an older Thad. He was a little annoying, wasn't he? Was he going to get worse with age? No, he wasn't. People grew softer and gentler with age, when they acquired wisdom, when they raised children, when they experienced love.

Just because Hudson sounded wise didn't mean that everything he said was gospel.

Chapter 10

Hudson wasn't nervous yet, but he was surprised that he hadn't heard any rescue efforts outside. Every few minutes, Louis Pasteur would check in with them, but other than him, they hadn't heard from anyone. He hoped the people in the bathroom were faring as well as he and Evelyn were.

Evelyn fidgeted beside him.

"How are you doing?" he asked. "How is your ankle?"

"It hurts, but I'm okay."

"Are you hungry? I can probably find you something other than raw carrots."

"You mean some honeydew?"

"With a little effort I might be able to do even better than that."

"I don't doubt it, but no, thank you. I'm okay. I think I'm in a little too much pain to be hungry."

"How about thirsty? Do you want something to drink?

She looked around. "Do you see any drinks?"

"No I was going to juice some of those carrots for you."

She giggled. "Oh please no."

"Are you sure? Add a little ginger, maybe a little apple, and carrot juice is delicious."

She gave him a bewildered look. "Are you serious?"

"Serious about it being delicious, absolutely. Serious about juicing carrots for you in the cooler? That was a joke. I saw some orange juice over there." He pointed with his chin.

"Orange juice sounds amazing."

He hopped up and grabbed a bottle from a box. "Do you mind drinking out of the jug, or do you want me to look for something to use as a glass?"

She took the jug out of his hands as he talked. "This is fine, thank you."

He settled in beside her again. He really wished he could do something about her ankle.

She didn't open the orange juice.

After a few minutes he said, "I really will look for something to use as a cup."

She insisted that she was fine. "I'm happy to haul off the bottle." She chuckled. "It's embarrassing, but I just got to thinking, maybe I shouldn't drink anything."

And then he knew what she meant. "Oh no. You're right. But please know that if it comes to that, I will do everything in my power to give you some privacy."

"Thank you. I appreciate that, but let's hope it doesn't come to that."

He was torn. He didn't want it to come to that either, but he was also really enjoying being trapped in there with her.

Louis started barking again, and this time he didn't stop.

"Someone must be out there this time," she said.

He got up and went closer to the smashed in wall, straining to hear anything other than the barking. He didn't, though.

And then the barking stopped, and he heard his name. It was so faint, he wondered if he'd imagined it. "Chase?" he shouted. Hudson heard his name again. "Chase?" he shouted as loud as he could.

"Yeah ... here." The reply was frustratingly faint. "... right?"

Hudson guessed at what he was saying. "People are trapped," he yelled and then winced. Maybe he shouldn't have said that. He didn't know for sure that it was true. And yet he did, somehow.

"... on the way."

Hudson sighed. This was almost useless. Chase sounded a hundred miles away.

"Tell him to take care of Louis," she whispered.

He wasn't sure he could get that message across.

They didn't hear anything, neither canine nor human. Where had they gone? He didn't know Louis well and yet he was confident neither he nor Chase would have left.

Minutes ticked by, and then the compressor kicked on. Hudson returned to his spot beside her.

"I wish he'd bark again," she whispered after a long silence. She sounded so sad.

He longed to comfort her, but he didn't know how to do that without taking her into his arms, and he was pretty sure she didn't want him to do that. "I'm sure he's fine. Chase would never leave a dog out there."

"He's your brother?"

"One of them, yeah."

"How many do you have?"

"Five."

"Good grief. Any sisters?"

"Nope. Much to my mother's dismay."

"Well good for her for stopping after six. That's a lot of kids."

Hudson wasn't sure she'd stopped on purpose, but he didn't say that.

"And how many of you live at the ranch?"

"Just Chase and me. But the others are there a lot, except for Burke. He's on the road a lot."

"Is he a truck driver?"

"No, he's a bull rider."

"Seriously?"

"Yep."

She looked at him quickly. "You don't approve?"

"I don't disapprove. I just worry about him."

"Oh, you're a good brother then."

"I try."

"So you and Chase host weddings?"

"Not yet. But we're trying. Did you hear about that little Mindy Rose show we had?"

"Who didn't?"

Her response pleased him. "Yeah, that was a big deal for us. Since then, we've been busy. And we're booked out for months but no weddings yet."

"That's sad. I like weddings."

He'd never thought about it, but hearing her say that made him say, "Yeah, I do too."

"So what kind of bookings?" she said quickly, as if she were eager to stop talking about weddings.

"Parties, a family reunion, a women's retreat, a—"

"A women's retreat?" she cried, and he relished the jealousy in her voice. She must have known it was there because she hurried to say, "So your brother is a dog lover?"

Hudson bit back a chuckle. "Yeah, Chase loves all animals."

"Good. That's comforting."

Oh good. He'd managed to comfort her after all. Or at least Chase had. "Are you cold?"

She hesitated and then nodded. He put his arm around her, pulled her tight, and briskly rubbed her arm. "If you get too cold, we can always bury ourselves in cabbage leaves."

She laughed. "How comfy." The compressor kicked off again. "Good," she said. "I wish it would stay off." Seconds later she gasped. "Did you hear that?"

"No." He concentrated, and then he did hear it. Shouting. "Voices. A few of them."

"Yeah. Maybe the calvary has arrived."

He didn't think so. He hadn't heard sirens. Maybe they'd been buried by the cooler's noise, but he doubted it. Sirens had a way of piercing through other noises.

The voices stopped, and then a much louder voice busted through the quiet. "Help is on the way," a man said and then repeated himself two more times.

"What was *that*?" Evelyn asked when he fell quiet.

"I'm thinking someone found a bullhorn."

"Oh." She exhaled, sounding relieved. "That makes sense, but where is the help coming from, Mars?"

"Maybe Whitewood or Deadwood?"

"I think those people would be here by now. Those towns are close. Well, South Dakota close, anyway."

She had a point. "I don't know. There must be other people who needed help. It's too bad we don't have a deck of cards." He looked at her, trying to give off a playful vibe, which really wasn't his thing. "How about a game of charades?"

She laughed and then winced.

"Seated charades, of course."

"Either it's stiffening up, or my adrenaline has worn off."

"Here. We should have already elevated it." He hopped up to find something soft to prop her leg up on. At first he couldn't find anything suitable, but then he dug through the pile of packages that had fallen off the shelves. "Jackpot!" He held up a giant bag of cheese, the weight of which surprised him, and he almost dropped it. "Tell me, why would they ever need a bag of cheese this big?"

She laughed. "I don't know. They don't have a salad bar."

"That's it. They *do* sell premade salads." They were absolutely terrible, but somehow, they still sold them. He stood and crossed the small space to her. He went down on one knee, balancing the giant cheese bag on his leg as he gently picked up her injured foot. Then he clumsily moved the cheese bag to the floor, where it landed with a splat that made her giggle. He lowered her foot onto it and then fell into disappointment. "That's not high enough."

"Is there another garbage bag full of cheese?"

He laughed. "I'll go look." He went back to the pile of food.

Chapter 11

Chase tried to call the basset hound away from the rubble so he wouldn't be in the way of the fire department, but the hound was a single-minded soul. Chase couldn't get too upset about this; he could be pretty single-minded himself. The dog had mostly given up on his barking and instead now whined and pawed at the pile of cement, desperate to move chunks far too big and heavy for his chunky, clumsy paws to move.

Chase didn't know the men taking over the scene, which meant they were from a neighboring town. He tried to read the side of the fire truck, but he didn't have a good angle. He would find out later. One of them barked some orders, looked at the dog, and then looked at him expectantly. The hound wasn't Chase's dog, but apparently he was for right now. And if they didn't find good things under this mess, then maybe the dog was his for good. He really hoped it wouldn't come to that. He hoped everyone under that mess was alive and well, and if he did need to adopt the dog, it was going to cause a fracas.

Hudson was allergic to dogs.

Chase undid his belt buckle, pulled his belt off, and then went for the dog. He couldn't quite reach him, and he didn't want to climb up onto the rubble in case it wasn't stable enough to support his weight. "Come on, buddy," he said quietly. "You have to do this for your master."

The hound stopped whining, looked at him, and tilted his head.

"That's right," Chase said gently. "It's just for a minute. Come here, buddy."

At first he didn't think it was going to work. The dog broke eye contact and pawed at the pile some more, but then after one final whine, he surrendered and came to Chase, who scooped him up in his arms and carried him off to the side. The dog kept his eyes riveted on the spot he'd been standing on. Chase set him down gently and looped the belt over his head. "This is just for show, bud," he said quietly. "So they don't worry about you getting in the way. I know you wouldn't do that, right?" He patted the dog on the head and then straightened to watch.

A delivery truck had been blown onto the roof, but it hadn't stayed there long. There was only a small dent in the roof, and then the truck had slid down the side, and now some of its weight was on the ground. Some of its weight, though, was resting in the divot it had created in the side of the building. And they were hooking the winch to the back of the truck, which was the part that was resting on the ground. This didn't seem right to him, and he tried to figure out why.

Then he knew, and he yelled at them to stop, but they couldn't hear him. He dropped his belt-leash to wave with both hands, but no one saw him, and then there was this sickening scraping sound followed by the loud collapse of that part of the building.

Mid-collapse, the dog started to bolt. Chase dove for his belt, landing flat on his stomach in the dead grass like some kind of heroic shortstop. His fingers found the end of his belt and he pinched tight before scrambling to a seated position and pulling the frantic dog into his chest. "I'm sorry, I'm sorry, I'm sorry," he said, holding the dog tightly.

The hound had trusted him. Had trusted these humans to help. And look what they'd done.

Chase couldn't look. He didn't want to see. His whole body shook, and sweat poured out of his pores. *Just breathe. Just breathe.* One breath in, one breath out—everyone was shouting—one breath in, one breath out—he could still hear things falling—one breath in ... Finally calm enough to look up, he saw the damage.

He didn't know exactly where Hudson was located, and all of the rescuers were scurrying around and not actually doing anything.

Coming back to himself, he got to his feet, stood tall, and headed toward the building. The hound ran beside him, barking his head off. Chase waved at a fireman to turn the truck off, and then he waved at the others to stop shouting. He bent to pat the dog and ask him to stop barking, but he didn't need to ask. When everyone else fell silent, so did the hound.

Chase stood up straight, looked at the rubble, and listened.

He listened for some sound that would suggest that his brother was still alive.

And the hound listened too.

Chapter 12

Wow, this man is so sweet, Evelyn thought.

Hudson returned to Evelyn with a smaller, but still significantly sized, bag of cheese. "How do you feel about feta?"

"I prefer it with pepperoni, but sure."

He tried to hide it, but he was obviously disgusted.

"Oh yeah, that's right. You're a health nut, aren't you?" She'd seen him in the cafeteria with his bowl of arugula.

"I don't think I'm a *nut*, necessarily." She picked her foot up for him, and he slid the bag under it. She carefully lowered her leg and sighed. This was incredibly uncomfortable, but so was the throbbing in her ankle, so if this would help, then she could live with it. "But I'm not as innocent as you think. I do have to eat pizza sometimes." He returned to his spot beside her.

She snickered. "*Have* to?"

He nodded, looking completely serious. He turned his head to look at her. "Emotional reasons." He was probably joking, but this silly response made her fiercely attracted to him. She tried to look away and failed. "So, how about those charades?" he said.

She didn't know if he was kidding, but she did not have the self-confidence to play any type of charades with this man. She sighed. "How long have we been in here?"

"You just changed the subject."

I learned it from watching you. She tried to look innocent. "Did I?"

"Yes, and it's not the first time." He narrowed his eyes at her. "Don't think I'm not onto you."

She couldn't remember any other time she'd changed the subject with him, and she didn't know why she suddenly felt feverish. She tried to be dainty as she dabbed at her forehead.

"I don't know how long we've been here," Hudson said. "Probably not nearly as long as we think."

She groaned. She needed to get out of there. Where was that rescue team?

He took his glasses off, tipped his head back, closed his eyes, and rubbed the bridge of his nose. He was handsome enough with his glasses on, but when he took them off—she tore her eyes away.

A new sound broke through the faint shouts outside. "Is that ..."

"A siren."

They both fell silent as the sound grew closer and closer until it suddenly shut off. In the distance there was more shouting, which grew louder until it sounded like the men were right outside the cooler. This brought Evelyn tremendous relief. Help had arrived. They would be out soon.

They sat there silently, together, listening to the sounds of rescue, which suddenly included a loud scraping sound. She gasped. "What was *that*?" It didn't sound good.

"My guess?" Hudson said. "Heavy machinery."

She looked up. Was the roof about to disappear? They wouldn't know because they were in a metal box. For all she knew, the roof was already gone.

The building around them moaned, and then the slanted cooler wall shifted.

"Oh no," Hudson said.

"What?" She tried to watch that wall, trying to understand what was happening, but she couldn't because Hudson was taking her into his arms and then he was lowering her to the floor. Oh no, not this again. She'd barely survived the last time without having wildly inappropriate thoughts. But yep, he was doing it again. His body was covering hers, making her feel small. His scent enveloped her—clean and woodsy. She tried not to notice how intoxicating that scent was. And why was he on top of her? Nothing was happening. Sure, the building was making lots of noise, but that wall had only moved a foot—

And then it happened. And it was so loud and so terrifying. She sunk her fingers into his chest and braced herself as the cooler collapsed in on them. Silently, she thanked God for a great life and prayed that everyone would live through this—

And then everything stopped. A few clunks echoed the crash, but it felt quiet in comparison. She blinked her eyes open, but there was no light. Great. She wished she hadn't taken that dim light for granted. Dust settled on her face, and she tried to blow it off her lips before realizing she was blowing up at Hudson's chin. She stopped. The debris could stay on her lips.

They were alive. She wasn't hurt. They'd survived a second cave in. But why wasn't Hudson moving off her? "Hey," she whispered, sharply aware of how close they were right now, how intimate this situation was.

"Yeah, I'm alive ..."

Was there a but coming? "Are you hurt?" she asked.

"I don't think so, but I can't move. I mean, nothing's crushing me, but when I try to slide off you, there's something in the way." He slowly turned his head. As if he was going to be able to see anything.

He was holding his weight up off her so he didn't crush her. That was going to become exhausting very quickly. "Let me try." She tried to shimmy to her left and made it about a foot before something sharp stabbed into her hip. She accidentally cried out.

"Are you okay?"

"Yeah, yeah, but I think that's as far as I'm going to be able to go."

He let his weight down onto his elbow, and then he was shifting his body to her right. He didn't move much, but it felt like it created significant space. He sighed. "There." He settled in beside her, on his side, his right arm still arched over her stomach.

"Well, this is cozy." Some of the dust fell into her mouth. It tasted like a refrigerator smelled. Not good, but she resisted the urge to spit the taste out. She slowly bent her knee to take some of the strain off her lower back, but that made her ankle hurt worse, so she straightened her leg again. The cheese had shifted a little and was now more comfortable. Or at least less uncomfortable.

"Well, it's a good thing the lights went out."

She could tell he was trying to be funny, but she didn't get the joke. "Why is that?"

"I'm not sure where my glasses are." He said this self-consciously, which she found odd. Not only was he gorgeous without his glasses, but they were now surrounded by pitch darkness. She couldn't see his face.

She got lost in thinking about his face until he interrupted her by asking, "How's your ankle?"

It wasn't good. "I'm okay."

"All right." He lifted his right arm off her and started exploring their surroundings with his hand. "Wow, I *cannot* tell what happened here. Too bad for you that you aren't trapped in here with my brother Wyatt. Seems you got the wrong Honeywood."

She was feeling some longing, for sure, but she wasn't longing for a different Honeywood brother. "Why, is Wyatt really good at fitting into small spaces?"

He chuckled, and she felt his chest vibrate against her right arm.

"I'm not sure about that, but he's a contractor. Spatial intelligence is his sixth sense. He would probably know exactly what he was dealing with here." He let his arm drop to his side. "But I have no idea. Feels like the cooler's roof, of course, but also like something broke through it."

"Like the roof, roof? The actual roof?"

"Maybe. I wish they hadn't knocked the roof in on us."

Her chest shook with a laugh that made no sound. "Yeah, me too."

"Don't worry," Hudson said, "Louis knows where we are." The affection in his voice was unmistakable. Affection for a dog he hadn't even met yet.

Chapter 13

Hudson's mind was spinning. He was working really hard to suppress his fear because he didn't want her to feel it. When he had to tell someone that they had cancer, he always made sure he sounded calm and confident. No one wants to hear the word cancer from a scared doctor. No, he always sent the message, *This is a tough situation, but you're going to be okay. And here's how.*

He tried to project that same energy right now, but he was struggling. He and Evelyn were in a tough situation, but they were going to be okay. He just didn't quite have the *how* yet. He knew how to fight illness. He didn't know how to escape a crushed metal box.

The dog had started barking again, and Hudson was glad for it. Not only was Louis doing the practical good of attracting attention, but his deep baying was providing Hudson with a steady stream of hope. Someone was out there. People were working on it. Help was there.

"Sorry," Evelyn whispered. "He's not usually such a barker."

Hudson couldn't believe she was apologizing for the behavior of Headache's dog. "No, I like it. I'm grateful he's working so hard." He laughed softly. He couldn't believe how much he was looking forward to meeting this dog. *Don't get too attached*, he warned himself. Not only was he allergic to dogs, but this wasn't even her dog. It was Drake's.

The allergies he could overcome. He wasn't sure there was a pill for Drake.

Evelyn took a deep breath, and she sounded shaky.

"Are you doing okay? I mean, that's kind of a stupid question, but ..."

"It's not a stupid question, and under the circumstances, yeah, I think I'm doing spiffy."

"I think it's *spiffily*."

"Oh my word. You can't tell, but I'm rolling my eyes. And I don't think spiffily is a word."

"Pretty sure it is, but brave of you to argue when I can't prove you wrong."

"Oh, you think I'm going to forget about this, but I'm not. It's the first thing I'm going to do once I get to my phone, assuming my phone hasn't been dropped off in Oz."

He didn't get it. "Oz?"

"You know ... Dorothy and Toto?"

He chuckled. "Oh, right. Toto. The only dog to ever have a name worse than Pasteur."

"I'm not so sure that's true. I can say Toto without wincing."

"So that's the first thing you're going to do? Look up *spiffily*? Before you call Thad? Before you call your mom?"

She didn't respond, and his chest leapt with hope. Did this mean that she didn't want to call Thad? *Don't be an idiot. Talk about jumping to conclusions.*

The dog stopped barking.

"Hudson?" Chase's voice was still faint, but he sounded closer than before.

"Mind if I holler into your face?"

"Quick," she said before he finished the question. The woman really liked using adjectives where adverbs should be.

"Here!" he hollered. He held his breath.

Chase didn't make him wait for long. "You okay?"

"Yeah!" He didn't know for how *long* they'd be okay, but how to say that in a few words? "Trapped! Can't move!"

"Good job," Evelyn whispered, that small praise lifting him higher than he'd felt in years.

"Okay! Hang on. The dog knows where you are! We're coming!"

This information confused Hudson, but he didn't want to try to figure it out.

"The dog knows," Evelyn whispered, "but how did the dog tell the humans?"

Hudson laughed harder than the quip warranted, and he felt some of his anxiety leak out with the laugh. "Oh my gosh this situation is so absurd. Drake is going to kill me."

"I wouldn't worry about that."

What did *that* mean? That she was done with Drake? Or that he shouldn't fear a weakling like Lurch? He wanted to slap himself. He needed to stop making assumptions. "Maybe Louis is barking at a specific spot," Hudson said, "and so Chase is assuming that's where we are."

"Oh. That makes sense. I thought maybe he was a dog whisperer or something."

As if his ears were burning, Louis started barking again.

"More like a horse whisperer, but who knows how many animals he can communicate with." Hudson shifted his body.

"I look forward to meeting him. And to thanking him."

"Don't get your hopes up. He's kind of a grouch."

She laughed. "Really?"

Now he felt guilty for saying so. "Maybe not a *grouch*, but he's not a people person. He's a veteran, and his time overseas took a toll."

"Oh, that's right. I knew one of your brothers had served. I'm sorry that he's struggling."

"He's actually doing a lot better, but thank you."

They heard the rumble of equipment, and Hudson braced himself for more collapse.

"I was mad that it was so cold in here, but do you think we could get them to turn the A/C back on while we wait?" She chuckled at her own joke.

"At least the air compressor stopped turning on and off."

"Yes, at least we have that," she agreed.

Chapter 14

Chase stopped working for a second to survey the mess in front of him. A dozen other people were working just as hard as he was to clear the debris, and more people were joining every minute. On the other side of the building, a separate crew worked to get people out of the bathroom. Shouts of joy told him that they were getting closer to their goal than his team was. But their side hadn't had a delivery truck slide down the side of the building.

To their credit, the rescuers had pulled the truck off the building and were now working by hand to clear debris. No more big movements without thinking first, though Chase didn't think the building could collapse much further. If it did, it wouldn't be a building anymore, and he didn't want to think about what that meant for Hudson.

Chase wiped his brow and got back to work. Over and over, the dog got in Chase's way, and over and over Chase moved him aside. He wasn't irritated, though. He understood the dog's impatience.

Chase's fingertips were already rubbed raw. He had gloves back in the truck, but he didn't want to take the time to get them. So he just kept digging. Every few minutes, he would call out, and Hudson would call back. This didn't serve much of a purpose other than verifying that Hudson was still alive, but it also encouraged Chase because every time they hollered back and forth, Hudson sounded a little closer.

They were making progress. He was grateful this hadn't been a ten-story building.

Chapter 15

Evelyn could hear voices. Lots of voices. And constant movement. It had been a very long time since the second collapse, and she couldn't imagine how it was taking so long to get them out. What did it look like out there? How much stuff did they have to move? Were they in danger of another collapse? It felt like her thoughts were on speed, zinging around her mind, pinging off each other—causing her real anxiety. *And* she finally had to pee. It was a good thing she'd lasted as long as she had given how much coffee she'd drunk that day.

Apparently, Hudson and she had run out of things to talk about because they each lay there, side by side, silently. The entire right side of her body, from her shoulder to her foot, was pressed up against this man, and their small space was growing hotter by the second. She probably didn't want to know what the actual temperature was—it might scare her.

Hudson's even breathing beside her brought some comfort. She admired his composure, his resolute confidence that this was all going to be okay. It was contagious. She was pretty good in a crisis, but she didn't think she'd be nearly as calm as she was if he wasn't there beside her. She made herself focus on his breathing, in and out, in and out, almost like a meditation. If she focused on his breathing, her thoughts slowed down, made her feel less frantic.

"I have no feeling in my left butt cheek," he said.

Her laugh startled the rest of her, undoing a good deal of the work she'd done to calm down.

"I'm serious," he said, as if her laugh offended him. "If I don't move soon, I think I might do some real damage."

She had an idea then and instantly felt guilty that she hadn't thought of it before. "Here," she said and tried to roll onto her right side.

"No, no. I didn't mean that you had to move." He let out a short laugh. "I mean, where are you going to go?"

"It's not fair that I get to lay here flat on my back when you're all contorted. I'm sorry I didn't think of that."

"Goodness, always the nurse and worrying about other people's comfort. Why would you think of the blood flow to my butt? Don't be ridiculous."

Her whole body had stiffened up, and she was having trouble rolling over. She didn't want to push off on the hard rubble behind her because she didn't know what it was or what pushing it might do. So she buried the fingers of her left hand into his shirt and pulled herself onto her side.

"Ah!" he pretended to cry out. "HR! The nurse is trying to rip my clothes off!"

This made her laugh again, and she resisted the urge to smack him. Finally, she was on her right side. "Okay, try it now."

He scooched over, rolled flat, and let out the most satisfying sigh. "Oh wow, it's pretty sad how good that feels." He chuckled. "Thank you."

"You're welcome." But now what was she going to do? Lying on her side with nowhere to rest her head was really uncomfortable. How had she made him do that for so long? She tried to prop it up on her elbow, but small shards of debris drove into her arm. She tried to form her arm into a pillow so she could lie flat, but there wasn't quite enough room. She scooched down, trying to fold her legs in a bit to make room for her head, but she drove her ankle into something hard and nearly screamed. She was glad he was more comfortable, but what had she done? She stopped trying to adjust and focused on pretending she hadn't just reinjured her ankle. Her head lolled over her shoulder like someone nodding off in church.

"Here." He lifted his hand up and then, like a bad contortionist, bent his arm to get it behind her head.

Once she understood what he was attempting, she helped him by picking her head up and getting her arm out of the way. She'd thought he was going to give her his arm for a pillow, but then he pulled her into him, hooking his strong arm around her shoulders and then moving it down to tuck it under her left arm. She gingerly laid her head on his chest. And she'd thought they were intimate before. Ha!

He smoothed out her hair and then rested his hand on her shoulder. "Is that better?"

Oh boy, it was so, *so* much better. She realized something then, something she hadn't known before or hadn't let herself know. This man really liked her. And she didn't think that just because he was holding her. He would be this kind to any woman in this situation. That wasn't it.

She didn't know how she knew it, only that she did. So now the question was, what was she going to do with this new knowledge?

Chapter 16

Hudson held onto Evelyn, constantly reminding himself that this was probably the last time he was going to get to do this. Chase and the others were clearing the debris, and though it was taking quite a while, the sound of their work was getting louder, which meant they were getting closer. Soon Evelyn would be free, and she wouldn't need him anymore. She would go back to her old life. With Drake and Louis.

"Bet you're wishing you kept your cushy job at the cancer care center right about now."

"Why's that?"

"Uh, so you wouldn't be buried in tornado debris."

"Oh, that. I'm sure it's possible for a tornado to hit Rapid too."

"Maybe." Though he'd never heard of one. "I'm surprised you had the day off today."

"Yeah." She didn't sound happy about it. "I think Thad pulled some strings."

"Oh yeah? So he could send you to the grocery store?" He felt her stiffen and hurried to say, "So you moved from Rapid to West Hope just to be closer to Dr. Drake?"

She hesitated. "Yeah ... and the new job ... and Louis."

He gave her a moment to offer an explanation. "But you took the new job to be closer to Dr. Drake?"

"Yes ... and Louis."

"Did you like working at the cancer care center?"

"I did. I loved it, but it was also hard. It was stressful. I thought that moving to a small-town hospital and more time with Louis would make my life less stressful."

"And did it?"

"Yes, but more time with Thad is stressful, so it all balances out to be the same as before."

Hudson laughed and then felt guilty because her head bounced up and down on his chest. "Sorry. You surprised me with that admission."

"Yeah ..." She sounded tired.

"Hey." He shook her gently. "You doing okay?"

"I am." She made her voice stronger. "Sorry. I'm just ..."

"It's okay. Just wanted to make sure you weren't feeling weak or anything. If I've misdiagnosed you, I won't be able to live with myself." He felt a silent giggle travel through her. "Well, I'm glad you like it at the hospital. I'm sure people like having you there."

"I'm not sure Thad likes having me there," she said softly.

Her words made his heart ache, and he was desperate to comfort her. "Aw, I wouldn't think that. You couldn't know this before you got there, but Drake is a major pain in the butt to everyone there, from the volunteers up to administration. Why do you think they call him Dr. Headache?"

Her quick intake of air told him that this was the first time she'd heard the nickname. He waited for her reaction and because he was expecting her to launch a verbal defense, it took him a second to realize that she was giggling.

She was *giggling*? What on earth did that mean? He almost felt defensive for poor Dr. Headache.

Almost.

"What's so funny?"

"I'm sorry." She sucked in some air. "I didn't know that." It was obvious she was trying to regain control of herself. She'd been in this small space for too long. It was messing with her head. She slowed her breathing, "Sorry I really shouldn't be laughing."

No kidding. He could judge her for it, but he couldn't really blame her.

"Okay. I'm done." Another giggle bubbled out of her, but then she did stop. "Sorry, I think I just experienced some stress release."

"Feel better?"

"Actually, yeah, I do." She sighed. "Well, that's sad to hear. I'm not exactly proud to be with a man who gives people migraines. I'll see if I can help him with that."

Oh great, she was going to try to fix him. Not exactly good news for Hudson, but it wasn't his place to argue with her. Hudson made a decision then. He was going to kiss this woman. This was his only chance. Yes, it was wrong to steal another man's woman, but he was going to try. God had allowed them to be trapped in this strange situation together. Maybe it was a test.

Or maybe it was a gift.

Chapter 17

"I can feel you judging me," Evelyn said softly. She let her eyelids drift shut and laid her open palm on his chest beside her face. His warm chest continued to rise and fall with his calm, even breaths. If it weren't for the throbbing in her ankle and bladder, she would be quite comfortable.

"I don't know what you're feeling," he said slowly, "but it's not me judging you. Unless by *judging*, you mean judging that you are utterly amazing."

"I'm not, though." And where had he gotten that idea? She was so ordinary that it pained her.

"You are, and I wish I could make you know that ..." It seemed he had more to say, but his voice trailed off.

Something deep, deep within her responded powerfully to those words. She was feeling something new, and she wasn't sure it was a healthy feeling, or a safe feeling. This man thought she was special, but what did that mean, really? To be special meant that she was different from others, right? But she wasn't. She wasn't any better than anybody else, and to think that she was could only invite trouble. "I'm not the angel you think I am," she heard herself say, desperate to convince him that she wasn't worthy of whatever he was feeling. "I'm divorced, you know."

She expected him to react, to laugh, to recoil, to do something, but he didn't move. His chest rose and fell at the same rate. "I didn't know that. I'm sorry you had to go through that."

She wanted to protest, to say she wasn't the victim, to say she didn't deserve sympathy, but part of her knew that wasn't true, and it was that part of her that sent hot tears to her eyes and kept her from saying anything.

"How long were you married?" he asked quietly.

This question had been asked and answered so many times it took no effort this time. She didn't have to think, and there was no emotion attached. "Six long years." Again, she expected a chuckle, and again she did not get one.

"What happened?"

"High school sweethearts. I don't know what went wrong, but he just turned mean one day, and that day came pretty quick after we were married, and then he kept getting meaner every day after that."

Now she felt his chest tighten.

"He didn't abuse me or anything," she hurried to say. "He was just really awful. He said awful things. He drank. He cheated. He smashed things. And then one day his awfulness maxed out, and he left."

Hudson exhaled. "Maybe leaving was a good thing then."

"It was." It had taken her a while to know that, but she did now.

"How long ago?"

"Two and a half years."

He stopped breathing altogether.

Why was *that* the detail that shook him?

"You've been with Drake for two years."

"Yeah."

"So did you date anyone between the ex-husband and Drake?"

Where was he going with this? "I did not." Why was her exact timeline so important?

His chest shook with a deep laugh, and he started breathing again. "Oh my word, Drake is your rebound."

Her irritation arrived swiftly and powerfully. "That's rude."

"What? Sorry, I wasn't trying to be rude." He rubbed her arm, which calmed her irritation so instantly that this caused her more irritation. If she could have moved away from him, she would have. "Wait, how was that rude?"

"You're patronizing me, suggesting that I would be in a rebound relationship without knowing it. Rebound relationships don't last for two years." She grew more indignant with each word.

"I'm sorry. I did not feel patronizing when I said it. I would never feel superior to you, Evelyn. Never."

That was nice to hear, and if it was true, then she needed to calm down.

"I was thinking about myself there, and I'm sorry. I've been wondering how a woman like you ended up with a man like Drake, and I couldn't figure it out. And then I thought I had some insight. I thought maybe your ex-husband was so terrible that he made Drake look good, but I shouldn't have made assumptions, and I apologize."

Her eyes grew hot again. He was right. But what did it matter how she'd gotten together with Drake? She still loved him.

Hudson squirmed, and she picked up her head to let him adjust whatever needed adjusting—something shifted, and more fine dust fell on her face. She closed her eyes against it and threw her hand up to wipe the dust off her lips—but her hand ran into the side of Hudson's face—and then his lips were on hers.

Gentle. It was so gentle. And then it was over. He had delivered the most tender kiss of her life, and then he had pulled away. She blinked her eyes open and was nearly blinded by the light. What on earth? Had that kiss cracked the heavens open? Was she seeing angels right now? Blinking rapidly, a gust of fresh air met her face, drying the sheen of sweat from her skin in an instant. She turned her face up to meet the blessedly cool air and saw clouds.

Beside her Hudson said, "They did it."

She turned her head so she could see his face, and dang it, wasn't it the most handsome face she'd ever seen. This cowboy-doctor who had been so good with her grandfather, who appreciated nurses, who made her laugh—he had protected her from a tornado and then he had sneak-attack-kissed her.

This was the most exciting day she'd had in a long, long time, and what she was feeling for him right now was probably just the adrenaline talking.

Probably.

Chapter 18

Hudson insisted they help Evelyn out of the hole first, and so by the time he was pulled out, Evelyn was flat on her back in the rubble with a large basset hound standing on her chest. *That* couldn't be comfortable, but Evelyn didn't seem to mind. Quite the opposite—she was smiling almost maniacally as the dog licked every speck of dust and every bead of sweat from her face.

A beautiful woman in a beautiful scene. It hurt to look.

He scanned the small crowd for Chase and found him hanging back. Chase was also watching the reunion, and he looked a bit like Hudson felt. Why would Chase be sad?

As soon as he'd asked himself the question, he knew the answer. While Hudson had been below the rubble bonding with the pretty nurse, Chase had been above bonding with the goofy-looking hound. And now those two were reunited, and neither had any further use for a Honeywood.

Chase looked up, met Hudson's eyes with his own, and gave him a tight-lipped smile.

Carefully, Hudson climbed down to go meet him. As he did so, he saw a crowd spilling out of the other side of the store. They all looked incredibly joyful—too celebratory to have lost someone.

Knowing Chase didn't like being hugged, Hudson offered him a handshake, which Chase accepted.

"Thank you," Hudson said.

"Don't mention it."

"I dropped your ice cream sandwiches."

Chase laughed. "I guess I can live without them for one more day." He pointed at Evelyn with his chin. "Is that her?" He blended the three words together into one: *Izzatur?*

"Is that who?" Hudson tried to play dumb.

Chase gave him some side eye. "The nurse. Cotton."

Hudson nodded. "Yeah, that's her." Guilt washed over him. She wasn't his to have, and he needed to come to terms with that *right now* before he really embarrassed himself and his family. She was taken. He'd given it the old college try; he'd kissed her; she hadn't kissed him back; and that was that. He looked at Chase. "How did you know?"

Chase shrugged. "Saw the way you were lookin' on."

Mental note to self: while he was recovering from her, he needed to stop being so obvious.

"Plus, you're right," Chase said. "She's beautiful."

"She is, but it doesn't matter. She wants to marry Thad Drake, and I want her to be happy, so if that's what she wants, then ..." He couldn't bring himself to finish that awful sentence.

Chase turned toward the parking lot, and Hudson followed. "That name sounds familiar," Chase said. "Who is Thad Drake?"

Hudson shrugged. "Nobody to you. He's from South Dakota, but not West Hope. I can't remember where. Probably somewhere east river. He's a doctor at the hospital."

"I've never heard you mention him."

"Yeah, he's really not worth mentioning. Certainly not worth marrying, but I'm not the one who's marrying him, so I guess I don't get a say." He knew he sounded bitter and wished he'd stopped talking several words ago.

Chase reached back and slapped him on the back. "Let's go get you a cold beverage. You want a ride? Not sure your truck is drivable."

Did that mean that his truck was still here? He scanned the parking lot, and what he saw made him feel queasy. Trash and groceries blown everywhere, several vehicles on their sides or roofs, a missing light pole. And while the wind had moved his truck, it still sat upright on four tires, and it was on the outside of the pileup, so if he could get it started, he could drive it away. "Let me try to get myself home. But thanks." He veered off to head toward his truck, knowing that he hadn't thanked Chase enough, but also knowing that Chase didn't care.

He climbed into the sanctuary that was the cab of his truck, tipped his head back, and closed his eyes. He was exhausted. He sat like that for a minute until a voice in his head reminded him that there were still a lot of people about. He sat up, shook his head clear, and pressed the button that might start his truck.

It worked, and he sighed in relief. He didn't know why he was so keen to drive himself home. Maybe because he felt more like a man if he did so. Maybe because he wanted to be alone. This brought a sharp pang of self-awareness. He often gave Chase grief for wanting to be alone. Now he understood it. He was overwhelmed by emotions and exhausted. Is that what Chase felt like every day? His eyes swept the parking lot looking for his brother. He found him sitting in his truck, staring at him.

Of course. Chase would sit there to make sure the truck worked. Better not to make him wait then while Hudson worked through his feelings. Hudson rolled his eyes at himself and put the truck in reverse. He backed out of the pile, put the truck in drive, and then coasted toward the road.

Good. Everything was working. A steady stream of vehicles were pulling into the lot, and Hudson stopped to wait his turn. He picked up his phone to start some music. He had dozens of missed calls and new text messages. Again he felt overwhelmed and vowed to deal with those later. He started his Mozart playlist and then crept out of the parking lot, weaving around evidences of the storm's damage until he reached the road, which was clear.

He had survived the tornado. He was free.

Chapter 19

Evelyn was starting to feel self-conscious. She didn't know how long she'd been on the ground celebrating with Louis, but she thought maybe she'd reached the limit of what was socially acceptable. Still smiling, she pushed him off her and sat up. She looked around for Hudson. She wanted him to meet Louis face to face, and she also needed to thank him.

But he was nowhere in sight.

Trying not to limp, Evelyn went fifty feet from the building and stopped. She'd been heading to the car like it was any other day, like her car would just be where she'd left it when she came out of the store.

But this was not any other day. Her car was a few spaces over from where she had parked it and it was flipped on its side. She looked down at Louis in horror. What had she put him through? Even though she'd already petted every inch of him, she knelt right there to examine him for injury. Had he been cut, hurt? She applied pressure over every inch of his body to see if he would whine or cry out, but he just kept wagging his tail, his eyes smiling up at her. He had no idea why she was suddenly giving him a deep tissue massage.

She straightened and put her hands on her hips, looking at the car. Now what was she supposed to do? Her phone was in the store. And even in small town, South Dakota, pay phones had gone the way of the telegraph. She turned and looked at the crowd, scanning the faces for someone she knew, someone she could borrow a phone from.

Where had Hudson gone? He'd kissed her on the lips and then just run away? Why hadn't he stayed to make sure she was okay? Her offense was soon followed by guilt. He didn't owe her anything. He wasn't her boyfriend. He wasn't responsible for her. Why was she expecting him to stay until her needs were met? He had a life of his own to get back to.

"Come on sweetie," Evelyn said. "Let's go find someone with a phone." She hobbled back toward the grocery store, looking for a friendly face, and quickly became aware that she was not the only one in this predicament. A lot of people were standing around looking lost or staring teary-eyed into the parking lot.

She heard complaints that the phones still weren't working, but she also saw a few people talking into theirs. An ugly impatience snaked its way through her chest. She needed to get out of here.

She must have looked a fright because a paramedic approached. "Evelyn?"

She was touched that he knew her name and felt bad that she didn't remember his. "Hi," she said lamely.

"Are you okay? Have you been seen too?"

"I'm fine," she said avoiding the second half of the question. "But I sure could use a phone so I can get a ride home."

"Happy to let you try my phone, but it hasn't been working. You know what? I could get on the bus radio and ask them to call Dr. Drake?"

This didn't bring her the surge of joy that it should have, which depressed her further. "That would be very kind. Thank you." She hated the quiver in her voice.

He was looking at her feet, and she shifted her weight so it would be evenly distributed to both legs. She tried not to wince and failed. "Are you sure you're okay?"

"I'm sure."

"Would you like to sit in the bus while you wait? Or until I need to drive it away, anyway?"

The offer was tempting, and even though Louis probably wouldn't panic if she sat in the front seat of the ambulance with the door open, she still didn't want to do that to him. "No, thanks. I'm okay." She watched him walk to the bus and then limped to the edge of the parking lot and sat on the brown grass. Louis lay down at her feet, resting his head on the toes of her left foot like he was Ruth, and she was Boaz. She giggled at the thought and then tipped her head back and sighed. She was emotionally tired. She needed a few hours alone with Louis to recover.

She put her hands behind her on the ground and reclined, resting her weight on the heels of her palms. But then she figured she might as well go the rest of the way and lay back, hooking her arm beneath her head for a pillow. This reminded her of how it had felt to have Hudson's arm around her, and her eyes grew hot. She closed them and took a deep breath.

You're going to be okay, she told herself. All of these crazy feelings were just a byproduct of the circumstances and the adrenaline. She was a committed woman. She was a woman in love. She was already in a healthy, established relationship. People didn't just change boyfriends the way they bought new shoes, on a whim, because they felt like it. At least, that's not how *good* people behaved.

She would go back to her old life, and everything would be fine. She decided that Louis was too far away, so she rolled onto her left side and patted the ground beside her chest. Lazily, he slithered up to join her without ever fully coming to a stand. Then he stretched out beside her, warming her from her chin to her waist. She rested her head on her left arm and hooked her right arm around his belly and then closed her eyes. She felt herself drifting off and didn't fight it because she knew she wouldn't fall asleep there on the ground beside a busy parking lot.

Someone was shaking her shoulder. She blinked her eyes open and looked up at them, squinting in the sunshine.

"Evelyn?"

The concern in Thad's voice made her belly flutter. See? He wasn't all flowers and precious jewels, but he did love her.

"Are you all right?"

She nodded and sat up, brushing her hands off.

"Then why are you lying on the ground?" His disgust was evident.

Self-conscious, she got up quickly, forgetting to keep the weight off her bad ankle. Pain shot up her leg, and she tried to focus on brushing the grass off her pants.

"What's wrong with your leg?"

"I twisted my ankle."

His face fell in what looked like disappointment. "Let's go get some x-rays."

"I don't need any. It's not broken."

"You can't possibly know that." The condescension was so thick that it made her skin crawl.

She pulled her arm out of his clutch. "I'm fine. I just want to go home. Can you give me a ride?" She looked down at Louis and changed her mind. She didn't want to go without him. Maybe she shouldn't go to her place then. She looked up at Thad. "Has anybody told you yet that Louis was a hero?"

Thad looked confused.

She nodded, trying to look cheerful in order to prompt Thad into cheer. She often had to give him emotional cues. "It's true. He told the rescue team where we were."

Thad turned to look at the building. "Why did he need to tell them anything? Weren't you in the tornado shelter?"

"Most of us were, but there wasn't room, so I was in the walk-in cooler."

He scowled. "You went to the walk-in cooler? You thought of that?"

His surprise was evident. Not to mention annoying. Had he always made a habit of calling her stupid? Or was this a new thing?

"Never mind. Can Louis come to my place for the evening?"

"If you don't want to be alone, why don't you just stay with me?"

She sighed. She'd never spent the night with him before. She wasn't about to start now. "Can you just give me a ride home, then?"

He didn't answer her, and she followed him to his car looking down at the tar so he wouldn't see her tired tears.

Chapter 20

Normally Hudson didn't mind Chase's potent introversion, but he minded it now. It seemed everyone that Hudson knew had received an invitation to come to the ranch to make sure he was okay. Chase, of course, was hiding in the horse barn, leaving Hudson to play host, but Hudson was too tired and too irritable to do so. He was physically exhausted, suffering the pain of unrequited love, and also feeling crushed by the weight of guilt. He had kissed another man's woman. He had done it with ill intent, which was bad enough, but the fact that it hadn't worked made it so much worse. He didn't know how he was going to show his face and he didn't know if he deserved to. If it weren't for the ranch and his family, he would already be packing to move to a new town.

Despite all this, he had to force smiles, answer the same questions over and over, and offer people snacks and beverages. And all of this with blurry vision. His back-up glasses were from his previous prescription, and they just weren't cutting the mustard.

He'd never been so happy to see Olivia come through his front door. He didn't know what she would do exactly, but he knew she'd be helpful, and he was right. She took one look at the chaotic kitchen, understood what was happening, and ordered him to go to bed.

"You really think these people are going to allow that to happen?"

"I will make it clear that you need your rest. Didn't you say you hit your head?"

He furrowed his brow in confusion.

"Exactly. You hit your head so hard that you don't even remember hitting it. But I will make sure that everyone knows it. So go lie down, and I will take care of this." She stared past him into the living room. "Do you want me to focus on keeping them happy and quiet or getting rid of them?"

He felt guilty saying it, but he said it anyway. "The latter, if you're able."

She nodded militarily. "Understood. I will be polite. They won't even know they're being gotten rid of. Now go."

Hudson kept his head down as he went to his room, avoiding eye contact and cursing the day he had complained that a crazy woman had driven her truck into the side of his barn. It was one of the best things that had ever happened to him. He was so grateful for Olivia for so many different reasons that this latest heroism was only a bullet point on a long list.

Hudson tried to rest. He really did, but not long after he lay down, a headache took root, and it quickly sprouted branches. Blaming it on the glasses, he got up to find some ibuprofen. When he got to the living room, Olivia and Chase were sitting together watching television. It was one of the strangest sights he'd ever seen.

Chase looked up at him. He didn't say anything, but Hudson could see his concern.

"I'm okay," Hudson assured him. "Just got a headache."

"I knew you hit your head," Olivia mumbled. Then, more clearly, she said, "Want me to get you something to eat?"

He looked into the kitchen and saw the dozen casserole dishes. "No, I think I'm okay." He headed for the medicine cupboard and found his pills. Then he made some herbal tea, found two cookies, and carried his feast into the living room. No one looked up at him when he sat down.

What on earth were they watching? Some sort of young adult soap opera. Hudson looked at his brother, expecting to see him grinding his teeth, but instead his expression was oddly slack—he seemed enthralled.

What was Olivia doing to their family?

Hudson ate one of his cookies and took an ibuprofen.

"Speaking of dogs," Chase said, and for a second, Hudson was quite confused. No one had said a word, let alone a word about dogs. But then he realized they were all being subjected to one of those commercials about homeless dogs. He really hated those. They always made him feel abjectly horrible. Commercials shouldn't be allowed to assault an unprepared viewer. Chase was looking at him expectantly.

"What about dogs?" Hudson said, nervous about whatever was going to come next.

Chase didn't answer him.

"You did some bonding today with old Louis, didn't you?"

Chase looked at him. "Louis?"

"The basset hound."

"Oh yeah," Chase said, his sadness so audible that Olivia looked up with concern. Chase chuckled. "Is he named after Louis L'amour?" His tone made it clear that he hoped this was the case.

The dog should be so lucky. "I don't think so." Hudson didn't want to go down that rabbit hole. He wanted to know what Chase was going to say about dogs. "So what about dogs?"

"I was thinking I could live in the barn. It's not really a barn anymore. Wyatt has fixed it up to be the nicest apartment within a hundred miles."

Hudson glanced at Olivia and caught her beaming with pride.

"And if I lived out there, I could get a dog."

"I didn't know you wanted a dog." Hudson knew that Chase liked dogs, but he thought he'd had his hands full with the horses.

"I didn't either. But now I'm thinking about it."

"Well, you can live in the barn if you want to." Chase pretty much did already. "But you can also live in the house." Hudson hoped this was still a possibility. "With the dog," he clarified.

Chase looked surprised. "But you're allergic to dogs."

Hudson nodded. "I am, but you're not the only one who grew attached to Louis today. I guess that's why God gave us antihistamines."

Chapter 21

The next time Thad kissed Evelyn, something was wrong. This made her feel terribly guilty. Did Thad's kiss feel weird because it *was* weird, or because Evelyn had kissed another man?

You didn't kiss him, she stuck up for herself. *He kissed you.* There was a difference. There had to be. But had she pulled away? She wasn't sure. It had all happened so fast. Yes, she thought she had pulled away. But had she done it fast enough?

When Thad went in for another kiss, Evelyn instinctively dodged it. She hadn't meant to, but she was actively thinking about another man, and her body followed her thoughts.

Thad pulled back a little. "What's wrong?"

You have to get a grip. This is your man. Not Hudson. Thad. No matter how good his arms had felt. No matter how safe he made her feel. No matter how his lips had …

"Evelyn?" Thad was staring at her.

"I'm sorry. I'm just feeling a little ..." How was she supposed to finish that sentence? She certainly couldn't tell him the truth. That she was distracted with thinking about another man? And not just any man, but another doctor who Thad felt he was in direct competition with?

"Out of sorts?" Thad offered.

She sighed. "Yeah, I guess." He wasn't wrong. She was certainly out of sorts.

He put his arm around her and pulled her closer to him. This felt nice, which further confused her. "I'm so sorry you had to go through that. It kills me to think of what could have happened to you."

His words surprised her. It was the most affectionate thing he'd said in a long time.

"I mean, I don't really want to admit this." He chuckled, and it sounded hollow. "But I don't know if I can live without you, Evelyn." He kissed her on the temple. "You've spoiled me. Now that I've had you in my life, I'm not sure I can do life without having you."

How was she supposed to react to this? How was she supposed to feel? She analyzed his words. They were nice words. They meant that he loved her. So she should be feeling loved. But she was feeling something else, and she didn't know what it was. She was confused, and she didn't like being confused. She was usually so self-possessed. Now she felt like she was being blown around by strong winds—completely out of control.

He shook her shoulder. "Aren't you going to say anything? I'm pouring my heart out here."

"Sorry. I'm not sure what you want me to say."

"I want you to say that you still love me."

She looked up at him sharply. "Of course I still love you. Why would you ask me that?"

He gave her a knowing look, but she didn't know what she was supposed to know.

"What?" Now she could add defensiveness to her swirling heap of confused emotions.

Annoyance flashed through his eyes so quickly that she wondered if she'd imagined it. "Didn't you just spend hours trapped in a small space with another man?"

She cast her eyes to her lap. "It's not like I did that on purpose."

He didn't say anything, but she could feel him staring at her. Finally, she looked up, and his eyes were wide. "Evelyn?" His voice was weighted with concern. "Did he do something to you?"

"What?" she cried. "Of course not!" She was hot with indignation. How dare he suggest such a thing about a colleague? "You know him!"

The concern slid off his face, and he studied her. He didn't say anything, but she could feel him accusing her all the same.

"I'm sorry, Thad. I'm just tired, and it's making me cranky." She wasn't cranky, but she thought saying so would placate him.

He slid away from her a little as he leaned forward and rested his elbows on his knees. Then he tilted his head to look at her. "Don't you think it's about time you moved in here?"

He always asked her this after they'd had a disagreement. She didn't understand his logic here. If he had any sense, he would shower her with affection and then ask her—but he hadn't tried that tack yet.

He was waiting for an answer.

"You know I'm not comfortable with that." She hated how sheepish she sounded. She wanted to sound strong and confident in her convictions, but she was so worn out.

"I know that you've said that, but I don't understand it. If you loved me, you would want to live with me."

"I do want to live with you." She was tired of explaining this. "But I want to do it as your wife."

"Fine. Then do it as my wife." His voice was matter of fact—emotionless.

She looked at him. "What?"

He smiled. "Yeah. Let's do it. You wore me down."

She didn't mean to, but she burst into tears. She stood up quickly, grabbed her coat, and headed for the door—she'd had enough. It was time to go home—but when Louis stood up and wagged his tail at her, she changed her mind. "I'm taking your dog for a walk." She went for the leash.

She didn't know Thad was behind her until he grabbed her elbow. "Hey, help me understand here." His tone accused her of being irrational. "You beg me to marry you, and then I say okay, and you erupt in histrionics?"

Something like rage churned inside her with such force that it took her breath away. She ripped her elbow out of his hand and flung the door open. He reached for her again, but she was already outside. Part of her wanted him to follow her, to know where he'd gone wrong, to beg her forgiveness—and part of her never wanted to see him again.

He didn't follow her. Of course he didn't. In his mind he hadn't done anything wrong.

She glanced down at Louis, who wasn't looking at her, but he didn't have his usual spring in his step. "Come on, honey." She tried to make her voice sound airy, but it was hard to work around the ire in her throat. "Let's get a move on." She tried to go faster, and still Louis only waddled along slowly.

She got in front of him and scooched down to get a look at his face. "Hey, sweetie. Are you feeling okay?"

He sat and looked up at her. His eyes always looked sad, so the sadness in them now didn't reveal much. She looked past him, at his house and its closed front door, and sighed. "I know, honey. I don't know what to do either. But for now, let's just walk. It'll clear our heads."

Chapter 22

Usually, Hudson was excited to go to church. This Sunday was not usual, though. He was still tired, and he had lactic acid built up in muscles that he hadn't used since high school football. He didn't know how he'd used them yesterday either, but apparently he had because he was some sore now.

But Hudson wanted Chase to go to church, and it was highly unlikely that Chase was going to go without him.

Hudson came out of his room, poured some coffee, and then went and shouted down the basement stairs.

Chase didn't answer.

Hudson looked out the window. He couldn't see him, but that didn't mean he wasn't out there. His truck was still there, so he was around. Hudson tried to drink his coffee as he walked to the door, sloshed some onto his clean shirt, and became unreasonably upset. He spent the rest of his walk wondering if he should change his shirt or just go with the coffee stain.

Chase was in the barn. He looked up when Hudson entered, and his eyes landed on the stain.

Yep, he needed to change the shirt. "Are you going to church today?"

Chase averted his eyes. "I don't think so."

"Come on, Chase. You need to go once in a while. It's good for you."

Chase closed the stall door and turned toward Hudson, still not looking at him. "I know that you think it's good for me, and I know your heart's in the right place, but not today." He walked by him.

Fine. Hudson tried to be patient, but he was annoyed. Now he had to go to church to prove a point. Maybe he'd stop and get a donut or two on the way. He never ate donuts, but they sounded good right now. He realized that he was self-medicating, and it wasn't the lame muscles he was trying to treat.

He was suffering from a bad case of unrequited love.

He changed his shirt, poured a second cup of coffee into a travel mug, and then went outside and climbed into his truck. At least Evelyn didn't go to this church. At least he had that going for him.

Chapter 23

Evelyn followed Thad into the sanctuary, and her eyes immediately fell on the unmistakable shoulders of Dr. Hudson Honeywood. He sat with his back to her, but there was no doubt it was him.

Of course this was his church.

And of course they would be visiting it today, the day after he'd held her in his arms and kissed her like a man on a mission.

This was the third church they'd tried since she had moved to West Hope. Thad hadn't liked the others. She slid into the back row and sat beside him. There were a lot of people here. Maybe Hudson wouldn't see her.

"Is that Honeywood?" Thad practically spat.

She didn't bother to feign surprise. "Yes."

He gave her a dirty look. "Did you know that he would be here?"

"Thad," she said, keeping her voice even, "you're the one who picked this place."

"That didn't answer my question."

She thought she'd answered it well enough, so she didn't say anything more. They still hadn't resolved the argument from the night before. She had dropped Louis off after a very long walk that hadn't cleared her head as much as she'd thought it would, and then she'd sneaked away.

She'd been surprised when he called in the morning to say, "I suppose you'll need a ride to church?" Then he'd suggested they try this place.

"Why did you pick this church?"

He shrugged. "No reason. It was the next one on my list." Thad didn't have a home church. He hadn't been a churchgoer since he moved to West Hope.

She, however, needed to have a church—*and* she was in a hurry to get married, so she knew they would need a church then. Might as well have one of their own so they didn't have to go hunting for a church that would marry two people they didn't know.

Hudson was moving. *Oh no.* He was getting up. She considered ducking down behind the pew in front of her, but then Thad would wonder why she was being so dramatic. He turned and headed up the center aisle. The closer he got to her, the hotter her cheeks burned. It was like some tortuous round of Hot, Hotter, Cold, Colder. Without the option to run away or duck down, she hunched over her phone as if she'd just received a particularly riveting notification.

Thad elbowed her hard enough to hurt. Instinctively she looked up to glare at him, and there was Hudson in all his glory. He offered his hand to Thad, who reluctantly took it. "Welcome! So good to have you here." Hudson let go of Thad's hand, and offered her the same greeting.

Feeling as though she were doing something wrong, she slid her smaller hand into his large, strong, warm one, and electricity shot up her arm with such force that she inadvertently pulled her hand away too quickly. Hudson noticed, and looked hurt. Oh great. Now she'd hurt his feelings on top of everything else. "Thank you," she said quickly, and when he looked confused, she added, "for the warm welcome."

He hesitated, studying her. Then he seemed to remember where he was. "Absolutely. Let me know if you have any questions or if you need anything."

She thought he was going to walk away then, but his shiny cowboy boots did not move.

"How are you feeling?" he asked. "How is your ankle doing?"

Absurdly she had the urge to tell him about the terrible fiasco she'd endured with her boyfriend the night before. Instead, she said, "Good." Then she sat there analyzing why she had the urge to tell the man she'd kissed about the fight she'd had with her boyfriend.

Because he listens to you when you talk, an annoying voice in her head offered.

"Good to hear it," Hudson said. He smiled at Thad. "Really. It's good to have you here. Please do let me know if I can be of service." He walked away then, and she missed him.

Thad groaned. "Well, this church is strike number three. Might as well leave now."

She looked at him, horrified. Was he serious? She couldn't tell.

"Are you the one who was in the tornado?" a young voice asked.

Evelyn looked down to see a cute little girl in the aisle looking up at her with wide eyes. "Yes, I was one of them." Evelyn smiled.

"Wow." The girl twisted back and forth, making her cotton dress swish around her knees. "Were you scared?"

Evelyn smiled and shook her head. "Not really. I tried to think good thoughts."

Someone called to the girl, and she ran away. Thad slid his arm around her shoulders. "That's my girl, always seeing the glass as half-full." So no, they weren't leaving, apparently. Evelyn's eyes filled with tears, and she closed her eyes and fought them back. She made herself think good thoughts.

Chapter 24

Hudson was a hero. Maybe even a legend. Every patient who came into his clinic wanted to hear all about how he'd saved the pretty nurse. He'd explained, again and again, that he hadn't really done anything, that God had done all the hard work, with some help from a basset hound and the fire department—but people didn't seem to believe him.

By afternoon—after a patient who complained of lower back pain while bouncing up and down; a woman who swore her smiling toddler had an ear infection; and a football player with knee pain that he couldn't quite describe—Hudson wondered if people were calling for appointments just to get an interview.

Even his brother Burke came in.

Burke never came in.

Hudson looked him up and down, wondering what the rodeo had broken this time.

Burke stiffly climbed onto the exam table, giving the paper a dirty look when it crinkled beneath him.

"You know, I've already told you the cure for what ails you."

"Yeah, and *I* told *you* that I'm not ready to retire yet."

Hudson sat and wheeled his stool closer to his brother. "How bad is the pain?"

Burke didn't answer, which was answer enough.

"You've been doing this for what ... fifteen years?"

"Fourteen," Burke said quickly.

"Burke." Hudson stared at him, willing him to be reasonable. He waited, giving him time to say something. "That's way longer than most people last." And Hudson knew that Burke's scores weren't getting better. They were respectable, but he wasn't improving. Hudson had never said it out loud, but he thought probably Burke had maxed out. He was good, but he wasn't the best. He'd gone as far as he could go. "There are other exciting things to do, things that don't take quite such a toll on your spine. You could jump out of airplanes or take up ice climbing?"

"I'm fine," Burke nearly growled.

"Then why are you here?"

A little life sparked in his eyes. "Oh yeah. So, maybe not so fine. So, I'm having trouble sleeping."

"Because of the pain?"

Burke nodded. Hudson knew that Burke didn't want an opiate prescription. He'd never taken them, been too afraid of getting addicted. "I can prescribe you something to help you sleep. It may just make you really tired, though, if you're in too much pain to fall asleep."

"It's worth a shot."

"Okay. And you're not on any other medications? Haven't seen any other doctors lately?"

"You're the only one for me, Doc."

Hudson chuckled and shook his head as he pulled out a prescription pad. Burke had been crazy good at math and science. He had so many options. Why he was so faithful to the rodeo, Hudson couldn't understand. He ripped the prescription off and handed it to him. "Is it the same pain you've been having all along or something new?"

Burke slid off the table. "I'm good. I promise."

Hudson grabbed his arm. "Have you had a new injury?"

"Naw. Just the same one over and over again." He waved the small piece of paper. "Thanks for the help." He started for the door.

"Burke, please listen to Ava. There's no shame in moving on to the next chapter of your life."

Burke turned and gave him a sour look. "Leave Ava out of this."

"Sorry, I just meant—"

"I know what you meant. And I'm not done with this chapter yet." He held up the piece of paper again. "Thanks for the scrip, Doc."

Hudson watched him go. He didn't know what to say. He didn't even know if he was in the right. He knew that Burke risked his life every time he went into the ring. But Hudson also knew that Burke loved bull riding more than most people got to love anything. Who was he to say that Burke should give up on his passion?

Even if Burke's way of life didn't make sense to Hudson, Hudson still respected him for it. He just felt bad for Ava. She had started dating a bull rider when she was a teenager. And then she'd married a bull rider when she wasn't much older than that. But now she was still married to one, and Hudson knew that she didn't find it much fun anymore.

Everyone knew that, and everyone felt bad for her. Everyone, except, apparently, her bull rider husband.

Chapter 25

Burke left Hudson's office furious. He was so tired of being judged by his family, and his physical exhaustion made that emotional exhaustion unbearable right now.

He had to get some sleep.

He pulled into the drugstore parking lot, winced as he got out of his truck, and then went inside. The little bell dinged over his head as he stepped inside, and the woman behind the counter looked up at him and smiled.

He made his way to her and handed her the slip of paper. She thanked him and invited him to have a seat. It would be just a minute. He did not have a seat. He wandered around the store instead, still stewing over Hudson's condescending attitude.

He paused to look at the magazines, and a dagger of pain shot down his leg with such force that he grabbed the rack to keep himself upright. It took his breath away, and he stood there frozen, waiting for it to pass. It did, but he felt like he'd been electrocuted. He took some deep breaths, let go of the magazine rack, and tried to stand on his own.

That's when he caught a teenage boy staring at him. He forced a friendly smile, but the kid still looked bewildered. "I'm okay. Just a twinge."

The boy nodded and walked away.

You just wait, Burke thought. *Time waits for no one.*

Maybe he should go sit in the small waiting area. Maybe that would be safer. Maybe he could even grab a quick nap. This thought made him chuckle, and he crossed the small store to the three black leather chairs in the corner. He smiled at the old man sitting in one of them, his cane resting on his knee, and then he slowly sank into another.

"Hey, aren't you Burke Honeywood?"

"I am."

"Hey!" The man grinned excitedly. "I saw you ride at Central States a few years back. You put on quite a show!"

Burke smiled. "Thank you. That's kind of you to say."

"Not kindness, young man. Just call 'em like I see 'em. You had a real talent."

Had? What did that mean?

"So how is retirement treating you?"

The question startled him. "Uh, I'm not retired."

"No kidding? Wow! Hard to hang up the spurs, huh?"

The woman behind the counter called the man's name, and he tipped his hat to Burke as he struggled to get out of his chair. Burke thought about helping him but then realized he wasn't moving much better than that guy.

The man checked out and then walked away without another look in Burke's direction. It seemed he'd forgotten he was even there.

Burke waited, watching the minutes tick by on the clock, listening to the buzz of the overhead lights. He tried to make them stop, but Hudson's words kept rattling around in his brain. *There's no shame in moving on ... way longer than most people last ...*

Hudson didn't understand. It wasn't about shame or pride or stubbornness. Rodeo was who Burke *was*. He didn't know who he'd be without it. Would he be anybody at all? Would he be nobody?

Listen to Ava, Hudson had said. Little did he know that Ava had stopped asking Burke to quit over a year ago. At first he'd thought she was finally understanding, but now he wasn't so sure. She'd grown distant. She used to act angry. Now she just acted detached, which was easier to ignore but somehow much worse than the anger.

He sighed and looked down at his calloused hands. The truth, which he wouldn't admit to anyone, was that he didn't know what to do. Was he losing Ava? If so then he had to quit riding. But he couldn't quit riding.

He heard his name called and was grateful to be distracted from his own thoughts. He would buy his pills, and he would go home and get some sleep.

This would all seem so much better in the morning.

Chapter 26

"How are you holding up?" Laurel Bannon asked Evelyn when the Monday morning emergency room action paused long enough to allow it.

"I'm fine." Had she given anyone a reason to think otherwise?

"I heard you were injured."

"Oh, just my ankle. It's already feeling better. It's amazing what some anti-inflammatories can do."

"Oh good. Next time you go grocery shopping during a tornado, you should make sure you have your Advil with you."

"Ha-ha," Evelyn said sarcastically.

"Good to hear that you're okay. I would imagine that an experience like that can really rattle someone."

"Oh, yeah. No, I had it pretty easy. Just me and Hud—I mean Dr. Honeywood in the cooler."

Laurel was giving her a knowing look, and Evelyn didn't like it.

"Don't go there." Evelyn tried to sound stern.

Laurel faked an innocent expression. "Go where?" She glanced past Evelyn, down the hallway, and stared for so long that Evelyn couldn't help but follow her gaze. Her eyes landed on Thad, headed their way. Evelyn looked away quickly and started to head in the other direction. "Wow," Laurel said, "running away from your boyfriend. Always a good sign."

"Do you mind?" Evelyn snapped, instantly felt guilty, and then quickly walked away before Thad could reach them. Her face was hot, and her eyes burned as she ducked into the break room for a breather. She never came in here—she rarely had time—and she didn't think Thad would look for her here.

She collapsed into a chair, tipped her head back, and closed her eyes. She didn't have time for this time out. There were people out there who needed her, but she really couldn't deal with Thad.

Last night had been rough. He'd started planning their wedding, even though she hadn't actually agreed to marry him yet. She hadn't had the courage to tell him to slow down. She wasn't sure she wanted him to. She wanted to be married, right? She wanted to marry him? She loved him. But the more he talked about the wedding they were going to have, about who they were going to invite, how they would honeymoon on the Las Vegas strip, the more annoyed she got.

Finally, she'd told him she had a headache and gone home without giving Louis his evening walk. It hadn't been a lie. Her head *had* hurt.

And then she'd come to work intent on avoiding her sort-of fiancé. What a mess. She was going to have to pull on her big girl pants and tell Thad what she wanted.

But first she had to figure out what she wanted.

She knew one thing. She had wanted a marriage proposal. A real one. A romantic one. She wanted him to *want* to marry her, to want to be her husband; she didn't want him to marry her because she'd "worn him down." What kind of a life would she have if he always looked at their marriage as some favor he did for her?

And she didn't want to honeymoon in Las Vegas.

But maybe she didn't deserve anything more than what she had. Maybe she was dreaming of pie in the sky. Who was she to demand a fairy tale ending? No one, that's who. Loads of women didn't get their happily ever after in real life, and maybe she wouldn't either. And it wouldn't be the end of the world. She could be content with the hand that had been dealt her. She could make the best of it.

She'd already had one chance at marriage, and she'd failed. She should be grateful she was getting a second chance at all. She needed to be content.

Yes, she decided, sitting up straight, it would be okay. She would *make* it be okay. She stood up and straightened her scrubs. It was time to get back to work and face her boyfriend, or her fiancé, whatever he was. She rolled her shoulders back, lifted her chin, and stepped back out into the busy hallway, just in time too, as she found out they were getting ready to move one of her patients to a room.

She hustled to catch up. "How are you feeling, Mrs. Hedderman?"

"Call me Chrissy." She coughed. "And I've been better."

"I'm sure you have been. But don't you worry. We're going to get you feeling good again soon." She pushed the bed down the long hallway as people stepped out of her way.

Soon she was helping make Chrissy comfortable in her own room.

Chrissy looked suspiciously at the empty bed on the other side of the room. "Am I going to have a roommate?"

"I can't answer that. Sorry."

Chrissy turned her attention to Evelyn's face, and Evelyn felt a little uncomfortable under that gaze. "Are you all right, dear?" she finally said.

"Oh, of course."

Chrissy continued to stare. She pointed at the door to her room. "You know, the door's closed. No one can hear you. If you've got something to get off your chest, now is a good chance. I probably won't even remember what you say, so I won't tell anyone." She chuckled and coughed again, and Evelyn offered her water, which she gratefully took. Evelyn thought the curiosity had passed when Chrissy asked, "Is it a man?"

Two men, Evelyn thought and then corrected herself. No, this wasn't about Hudson. He was a shiny distraction, but what was really bothering her was the situation with Thad.

"I was married for fifty-two years. It's a man. I can tell."

Evelyn paused her busyness to look at the woman. "Fifty-two years is a long time."

Chrissy shook her head. "Went by in a blink. You want to talk about a long time. The two years since he died. That's the definition of a long time." She smiled sweetly. "Come on, tell me what's going on in that heart of yours. Give an old woman a chance to be useful."

Evelyn returned the smile. "I think you're plenty useful just being you."

Chrissy rolled her eyes. It was adorable. A teenage expression on the wrinkled face. Made her seem timeless. "Fine then. Give an old woman a chance to *feel* useful."

Evelyn took a deep breath and glanced at the door. Was she really going to do this? "I was married too, and mine didn't go as well as yours." She paused, giving Chrissy a chance to respond, but Chrissy only waited patiently. "So he left me, and as painful as it was, I still thought, okay, now I get another chance to do it right." She didn't know where to go next with her story, so she stopped talking.

"So who's the man?"

Her mind jumped to Hudson, and her whole body grew warm. But wait, Hudson was not the answer to Chrissy's question. Thad was. "He's a doctor here. He's a good man, and I love him."

"But?"

Now Evelyn wished that she'd never started talking. She didn't want to be badmouthing Thad. In his hospital. To someone who could be his patient. She sighed. "You know what? There is no but. I'm sorry. I think I'm just overly emotional. Must be ovulating or something." She forced a laugh, and Chrissy didn't even pretend to smile.

"Oh, child. You need to tell someone. If it's not going to be me, you tell me right now who it's going to be."

Evelyn quickly flipped through her options. She'd had a good friend in Rapid, but she hadn't done a good job of keeping up with her since moving. She could talk to her mother, who would tell her to stop whining and marry Thad before he changed his mind. Her grandmother was gone. A sudden ache gripped her heart. How she missed her grandmother. Her grandmother would listen to her. She might not give her great advice, but at least she would be on her side.

She took a steadying breath and looked at the woman in front of her. The patient. She really shouldn't be unburdening herself onto a patient.

"You'd better hurry it up. I'm going to die of old age before you get to it."

That made Evelyn laugh. "There's not much to get to. I thought I wanted to marry him, and now that he's willing to commit, I'm not ... I don't know. I guess I just wanted to feel a little more ... I don't know. I'm sorry. I don't know how to explain it. I've just got a lot of doubts."

Chrissy looked contemplative. "May I be frank?"

"Please."

"You're a beautiful woman, so I hesitate to compare you to an ox, but I'm going to."

What?

"Imagine that you're an ox. You are pulling a lot of weight behind you. This *good* man, do you feel he is pulling in the same direction as you?"

Evelyn's gut said certainly not, but then she tried to reason with her gut. Maybe he was. Most of the time.

Chrissy shook her head. "His pulling is supposed to make *your* pulling easier. He's supposed to lighten your load. If his pulling is making your pulling harder, then sister, you really shouldn't make that yoke a permanent thing."

The meaning of her words washed over Evelyn with such force that she nearly staggered. "Wow. Thank you. You're a wise woman."

Chrissy smiled, activating a thousand fine wrinkles in her cheeks and around her eyes. "Thanks for noticing."

Evelyn finished getting her settled and then went to the door. She reached for the door handle resolved to break up with Thad. She could not marry this man. Anything this hard couldn't be meant to be.

But then she stepped out into the hallway, and an image of Louis flashed through her mind.

Oh no. What was she going to do about Louis?

Chapter 27

Hudson wanted to check on one of his patients who had recently been admitted to the hospital—Mrs. Chrissy Hedderman. She'd come to him complaining of back and chest pain, and he'd sent her to the hospital for some tests. They'd admitted her, so he was glad that he'd convinced her to go. On several occasions she'd made it clear that she'd had enough of this world and was ready to join her husband in heaven, but Hudson knew her grandchildren—and knew they weren't quite ready for that transition yet.

He sneaked in through the back door, going slowly, keeping an eye out for Evelyn. While he wanted to see her, he didn't want to interact with her. It felt too much like pain.

After a quick stop at the nurses' station to get Mrs. Hedderman's room number, he made it to her door without encountering anyone dangerous. He slid inside, and the woman's eyes lit up. "Dr. Honeywood! What a sight for sore eyes!"

He grinned. He couldn't help it. She was a charmer. Always had been. "Good evening, Mrs. Hedderman. I wanted to check in on you before heading home. How are you feeling?"

"I *feel* all drugged up, but other than that, I'm fit as a fiddle."

"Good, that's good to hear."

Her smile faded. "But you're nowhere near fiddle fitness, are you?"

The question surprised him. "What do you mean? I'm good." She didn't say anything, so he insisted, "Really. Life is good."

"Why aren't you married, Dr. Honeywood?"

Oh great. This again. "My mother always told me to wait for the right woman. I'm still waiting."

She nodded contemplatively.

He was suddenly in a hurry to get out of there. "So no more pain? Any trouble breathing?"

"You know, I'm not usually one to pry ..."

This was a bald-faced lie.

"But I happen to know about a beautiful young nurse who could use a good man like you to come in and sweep her off her feet."

Despite his resolve not to encourage her antics, his ears perked up. "Who might that be?"

She held up one hand as if to slow his excitement, which amused him because he hadn't thought he'd shown any. "Now apparently she's mixed up with someone else, but I can tell you that she shouldn't be." Her hand dropped. "I'm talking about Doug Cotton's daughter."

Hudson's stomach somersaulted, but he worked to keep a straight face. "You mean his granddaughter?"

Her face pinched in embarrassment, and he wished he hadn't corrected her. He hadn't needed to. He'd known very well who she meant. "Oh yes," she said. "Of course. His son's daughter."

Hudson avoided her eyes. There was a weird stain on one of the ceiling tiles right above Mrs. Hedderman's—

"What, do you not think she's pretty?"

"Oh ..." He cleared his throat. "No, you're right. She's very pretty."

"Good. So you'll ask her out, then?"

What a novel idea. Just ask her out. On a real date. Yes, she had a boyfriend, but he could still ask her out. What was the worst that could happen? She could say no, and he would be embarrassed, but it wouldn't kill him. He was man enough to tolerate a little embarrassment. And could the situation get any worse than it was?

"So?" Mrs. Hedderman was waiting for an answer.

"I'll think about it."

She narrowed her eyes. "Fine. If that's the best I can do. But don't think too long. If another good man walks in here, I'm going to suggest the same thing to him."

Hudson flinched. He didn't like the sound of that. "I'm glad you're feeling better, Mrs. Hedderman. You call me if you need anything." He started toward the door.

"There's something different about you."

He couldn't help turning back. "Oh yeah?"

"Yes. Are you doing something different with your hair?"

He chuckled. He'd had the same hairstyle since he was six. "No, ma'am."

"Then what is it?" Her gaze made him uneasy.

"I've got contacts in—"

"That's it!" she cried. "You're not wearing your glasses. So handsome! What's the occasion?"

"No occasion. I lost my glasses in the tornado."

She gasped. "The tornado sucked the glasses off your nose?"

He laughed. "Not exactly."

"I didn't realize you'd gotten caught up in that. Thank the good Lord that you're all right. Were you at the Pizza Ranch?"

"No, ma'am. I was at the grocery store."

"That's a good thing. I heard things got a little dicey at the Pizza Ranch. A tornado ..." She shook her head in wonder. "And all you lost were your glasses." She smiled. "But that's a good thing. You look great without them."

Didn't she realize that was the same thing as saying he didn't look great *with* them? "It's only temporary, I'm afraid. I've got new glasses on the way."

"No!" she cried with a disappointment that seemed over the top.

"Sorry. Contacts are uncomfortable, and I don't see as well with them." He edged toward the door. "Get some rest, Mrs. Hedderman."

"Yes, I suppose you do need to be able to see if you're going to keep saving lives"—he reached the door and wondered if he could walk out while she was still talking— "but do yourself a favor and wear the contacts when you ask Miss Cotton to go out dancing."

She couldn't see his grin. "Okay, ma'am. Good night." He left the room before she could say anything more, but he kept grinning all the way to the truck.

Only once he'd reached it did he realize he'd forgotten to avoid Evelyn on the way out. And yet he'd managed it. Phew. That could have been awkward.

Chapter 28

Evelyn yawned and recounted the pills. She didn't trust herself.

"Are you okay?" Laurel came up behind her.

"Good grief, you work a lot of hours."

"Not on purpose. Betsy is out on maternity leave, and they haven't replaced Allison yet, so they keep asking me to cover, and I keep saying yes."

"You should say no."

"I don't want to. They've been so good at working around Julia's softball schedule. I'm grateful."

Evelyn shook her head. "I don't know why you work at all. If I was married to a Bannon—" She looked up sharply. "Sorry, that sounded way snarkier than I meant it."

"No worries. People say it all the time. But this is part of who I am. I don't want to lose this part of myself just because I got married."

That made sense. What parts of herself would Evelyn lose if she got married? *That would depend on who you marry.* "Maybe I could take some of those shifts off your hands," she hurried to say. That would give her less social time with Thad, which would be a good thing.

Laurel was studying her.

"What? Why are you staring at me?"

"You look terrible."

Evelyn laughed bitterly. "Thanks."

"What's wrong?"

She shrugged. "Didn't get much sleep last night."

"Why's that?"

"I don't know."

"Yes, you do." She took the meds she needed. "But if you don't want to tell me, that's fine." She started to walk away but then turned around and came right back. "Okay, that's not fair. Meet me for lunch."

"Okay." Lunch seemed so far away that it didn't feel like a real commitment.

"Okay. Good. See you then." Laurel bounced away.

Despite Evelyn's doubts, her lunch break did arrive, but Laurel wasn't there. Evelyn was almost done with her salad, which she'd hardly tasted, when Laurel came running into the cafeteria.

"No! Don't leave!" She fell into the chair opposite Evelyn. "Spill it." She was out of breath. "I had to promise a million favors to get here." She rapidly slapped the table.

"There's nothing to spill, Laurel. I'm just ... Thad asked me to marry him. Actually, no he didn't. He said that he would marry me."

Laurel scowled. "What?"

Evelyn didn't say anything. She dropped her fork into her dish and leaned back. She was probably too tired to be working right now. "I know you're already too busy, but do you think you could cover me if I went and took a quick catnap?"

Laurel nodded, still scowling. "As soon as you explain what happened. He just said, 'Hey, I'll marry you if you want.'" Her impersonation of Thad's voice would have made Evelyn laugh if she wasn't too tired to smile.

"Not even. He just said, 'I'll marry you.' He doesn't care what I want." She felt guilty saying so. She really lacked a filter when she was this tired.

"I'm sorry."

Laurel's sincerity surprised Evelyn, who looked up sharply. She hadn't expected such empathy, especially without her providing more of an explanation first.

"I know that some men are really bad at being romantic," Evelyn said, "but they're still really good men who make really good husbands. You know, they provide for you and protect you and make good best friends … but I'm not sure that's what's happening here." Hot tears flooded Evelyn's eyes, and she hurried to wipe them away, but Laurel caught her hand and squeezed.

"Evelyn, do you want to marry him?"

She shook her head, annoyed that her eyes had turned into fire hoses.

"Then what's the problem? Tell him, *no, thank you.* Do you want to keep dating him? Is that what you're worried about? That he'll break up with you if you say no to marriage?"

She shook her head again and sniffed. "No. I'm not even crying about him." She tipped her head back and rolled her eyes at herself. "I can't believe I'm crying at all."

Laurel let go of her and leaned back. "I'm pretty sure you wouldn't be crying if you didn't need to cry."

Evelyn sighed, and she felt it in her whole body. Her tear flow began to abate. "I always cry more when I'm overtired."

"Yeah. Me too. But only if something sets me off first. So, Evelyn, tell me what set you off so I can help."

She shook her head. "It's embarrassing, and you can't help."

"Sweetie, *life* is embarrassing. Trust me. I was a young unwed mother in this small, gossipy town. I understand embarrassing, but I also know that it's never as big of a deal as we make it."

"It's the dog," she blurted out because it hurt too much to hold it in. "It's the stupid dog. I love him so much that ..."

"You love him so much that you're thinking about marrying a man so you can live with the dog?" She said this without judgment.

"Not *marry* him, but stay with him, yes. I don't know. It's like the blinders have been taken off. You know how you can be blissfully unaware, but then you learn something new and then you can't unlearn it? That's what this feels like. I thought Thad was good for me. I mean, he's a *doctor*. He's so successful! I changed my entire life for him. I gave up my job, I moved to a new place with a new job and no friends. And Thad has changed since I got here. He's not as nice, and I *hate* working with him. I had no idea he treated nurses the way that he does, and that makes me really disgusted with him. So yeah, I want to break up with him, but I can't because that dog is my best friend, and I know that this is stupid, and I know that he's just a dog, but he's not ... he's ..." She didn't know how to make Laurel understand.

"I don't like the phrase *just a dog*. It's not just a dog or a cat or a horse. They're living souls who trust us to care for them. So I get it. He's your loved one. But you know there are dog lawyers, right?"

She snorted. "What?" Like dogs who'd passed the bar or lawyers who worked for dogs?

"It's true. I know of one right in Rapid. Divorced people go through this all the time. Animal custody, though they might call it possession, can go to court."

"But we're not married." Maybe she should marry him and then divorce him to get the dog. She almost laughed at the thought.

"I don't know. I think you should talk to him." Laurel pulled out her phone. "I'll send you his link."

After her cat nap, Evelyn tried to do some internet research, which led her to believe that canine custody battles weren't as common as Laurel had let on. But the lawyer's website looked legit and specifically mentioned dogs, so, feeling like a fool, Evelyn hit the call button.

The attorney was in court and couldn't take her call, but when Evelyn said she just had some basic questions, the kind woman who had answered the phone said she might be able to help, and then she started asking some questions of her own.

By the time she'd ended the call, Evelyn was filled with hope. She and Louis weren't out of the woods yet, but she could see the clearing up ahead.

She hurried to find Laurel to tell her all about it.

Chapter 29

Hudson left the office and headed for the hospital still in his scrubs. He knew Thad worked banker's hours, and he figured Thad had managed to put Evelyn on a similar schedule, but he didn't know for sure, and he didn't want to miss her. He'd spent all day getting up his nerve. He didn't trust this bravery to last.

His eyes were on fire. His contacts were driving him crazy, and his eyes were so bloodshot he looked like he was at a Grateful Dead concert.

At first Hudson couldn't find Evelyn, and the thought that he'd missed her brought a weird mix of disappointment and relief. But then he saw her in all of her beautiful glory, hurrying down a corridor.

He hustled after her. There was no disappointment or relief now. There was only unbridled joy. Yep, he might be about to make a giant fool of himself, but it would be worth it just to be in her presence for another minute. Good grief. In her absence, he'd forgotten how madly in love with her he was.

"Evelyn," he said.

She turned to look, and her face lit up.

He took this as great encouragement. Then he got closer and saw her eyes. They were as bloodshot as his. "Hey, are you okay?"

"Yeah, yeah," she said quickly, dismissively. "Everyone's been saying it. I look terrible—"

"You don't look terrible," he interrupted. "I don't think you're capable of it."

Her expression softened. "That's sweet." She stared at him, and he lost his ability to speak. "I'm just really tired," she said to break the silence, which had become far too meaningful. "Been suffering a bout of insomnia."

"Oh." His brain leapt to possible treatments, but then he remembered that he wasn't there as a doctor, despite his outfit. "So, sorry to bother you at work, but I ... I didn't want to bother you at home either." He took a deep breath. "Evelyn," he started, surprised and a little impressed at the strength in his voice, "I am asking you out on an official date."

Her mouth fell open a little.

Anticipating a rejection, he hurried to change her mind. "I know you're dating someone, but I also know that you aren't married yet, and I'm asking you to go on one date with me." He made himself smile and then regretted it. His fake smiles always made him look a little unhinged. "Dinner and dancing." *Stop talking, you jerk.*

She kept staring. But she wasn't speaking. Maybe that was a good thing. She wasn't saying no. And she didn't look offended or angry.

But she didn't look excited either.

"Hudson, I have no right to ask you this ..."

Maybe she didn't have a right, but he still wanted her to ask any question of him that she wanted to.

"I like you," she said matter-of-factly.

Had that been a question?

"But can you be a little patient with me?"

There was the question. But what did it mean?

"Like I said, no right to ask that of you, but I would very much like to go on a date with you. But I just can't ... yet."

He was speechless.

She reached out and squeezed his arm. "I have to go, but thank you for asking, and if you still want to take me out when I am ready, I will be very happy about that." She hesitated, as if she wanted to say more, before letting go of his arm and walking away.

He turned to see Laurel watching him. He dropped his eyes and tried to get past her without chatting. He needed to process what had just happened, and he wanted to do that sooner rather than later, so he didn't have time for chit chat.

But Laurel wasn't going to let him get by. "Hey." She jumped into his path and looked over his shoulder where Evelyn had been. "What was that all about?"

It was none of her business, but he said, "I asked her out."

Laurel's eyes grew wide. She slapped him on the upper arm. "Good for you!" Her smile flickered. "What did she say."

"She said to be patient."

Laurel scowled.

"Right? What does that mean?"

"It's not you." Laurel looked around furtively and then tugged him off the beaten path.

He didn't know whether to be intrigued or annoyed.

After another scan, Laurel leaned closer to him. "It's the dog."

"Louis?" Hudson cried too loudly.

Laurel reared back, a bewildered look on her face. "The dog's name is Louis?"

"Sort of. What does Louis have to do with any of this?" He knew he sounded defensive of the pup, but he didn't know how to stop it.

"Do you *know* this dog?"

"What about him, Laurel?"

"Okay." She looked around again. She was a nurse. Talking to a doctor. In a hospital. Who did she think was going to catch her? And what did she think they were going to catch her doing? She was acting like she was in some low budget spy movie. "The dog isn't her dog."

"I know that."

"Oh. Well, *excuse* me. I didn't know that you were best friends with this dog." She must have seen his exasperation because she continued. "Anyway, she wants to break up with Dr. Drake, but—"

"She told you that?"

"Will you keep your voice down!" Her eyes darted around again.

Oh. So that's what she was worried about. No wonder. She didn't want Drake to catch her meddling in his personal life. "Sorry. Go on."

"So she talked to a dog lawyer, and she—"

"She talked to a *dog* lawyer?" he cried. There was such a thing as a dog lawyer?

"Yes, she didn't know that they existed either. I told her to call. Anyway, will you just listen for a second, please?"

He blinked. He hadn't known Laurel could be so sassy. Amused, he stared at her expectantly.

"Okay, so someone at the lawyer's office suggested a plan, and I think she's going to go with it. But it will take a while. That's why she asked you to be patient."

"What's the plan?"

Laurel looked hesitant.

"You can tell me the plan. We're talking about a dog here. This isn't exactly personal."

"Yes it is," she snapped. She took a breath. "I think the plan is that she takes Louis home. He stays with her for a while. Then she breaks up with Dr. Drake, but because Louis has been with her, she should be able to keep him."

"What? That's a terrible plan!"

Laurel looked personally offended.

"It's going to take too long! And is there any guarantee it will work?"

Laurel didn't know.

So that was a no. There was no guarantee. She wanted to break up with him. That was great news, but she was going to drag this out and make their relationship die a slow death. Bad news.

He sighed. "Okay. Thanks for the info."

"You didn't get it from me."

He didn't agree to that, but neither was he going to create drama on purpose.

He walked out of the hospital close to fuming. Why was Drake such a jerk? He didn't even like the dog. He couldn't just let her take it with her?

Think, Hudson. He was an intelligent man. Surely he could think of a solution to this problem that made more sense than the one the lawyer had given Evelyn.

Maybe Hudson could offer to buy the dog. He didn't know Drake that well, but he knew he wasn't starved for cash. And Drake knew that his girlfriend loved the dog, so he probably wouldn't be willing to sell it.

Hudson stopped walking and stared at his truck. He had to try. He turned, scanned the lot for Drake's car, saw it, and then headed back inside.

By the time he found Drake, he'd almost lost his nerve.

Drake looked at him suspiciously, and Hudson summoned a picture of Evelyn into his mind for motivation.

"What can I do for you?"

"My brother has decided that he wants a basset hound"—Drake narrowed his eyes—"and I'm kind of partial to the breed since yours rescued me from a demolished building."

Drake rolled his eyes. "You sound like Evelyn. That dumb dog did not rescue anyone."

Hudson worked to look impassive. "Anyway, my brother hasn't been able to find a basset hound locally"—to Hudson's knowledge, he hadn't tried either—"and Evelyn mentioned that you weren't a big fan of dogs."

He cocked one eyebrow. "Oh, she did, did she?"

"Yes, so I was wondering if you wanted me to take him off your hands."

Drake grimaced. "The dog is a thoroughbred."

Hudson winced. Good thing Chase wasn't here. Drake's misuse of the word thoroughbred would have really set him off. "Sure, I would pay you of course." He'd thought about throwing out a number, but he didn't have a good one. He wanted to go high enough to tempt the man, but not high enough to make him suspicious. If he offered ten grand for a dog, surely Drake would suspect something else was going on.

Drake named a number. It was ridiculous. The poker face was getting harder and harder to maintain. "I haven't done any research about what they cost, but sure. That works for me." He held out his hand to shake on it.

Drake pinched his face and stared. "Not so fast."

Hudson's hand dropped. Now what?

Drake's face said it all. He'd asked for too much money, and Hudson had stupidly agreed. Maybe he wasn't as smart as he thought he was. "Why do you want this dog so bad?"

"I told you. My brother wants it."

He shook his head. "You're full of it."

Hudson could see his wheels turning, and he grew nervous. Drake wasn't stupid. He was going to figure this out, and then Evelyn's plan wasn't going to work. He had blown it.

"I don't know what you're up to Honeywood, but I know you're up to something. Tell you what. You let me work for your little group practice, and I'll give you the dog for free."

Of all the things that could have possibly come out of this jerk's mouth—Bible verses, Taylor Swift lyrics, or Latin poetry—this was the last thing Hudson expected to hear. He just wasn't imaginative enough.

"Well? What do you say?"

Hudson didn't know what to say. His family practice was busy. They could absorb another doctor, but not *this* doctor. "I'll talk to my partner," he heard himself say.

Drake smiled. "Great news. When I get the job, you get the dog."

Chapter 30

Evelyn slammed her locker and headed for the hospital's back door. As usual, Thad wasn't waiting to walk her to her car. He'd already driven away, expecting her to follow him to his home like the obedient little minion he believed her to be.

At least that's what she thought. Until she stepped outside and saw him leaning on his car.

She could feel his anger from fifty feet away. "What's wrong?" She stopped short, not wanting to get too close.

"Do you two think I'm stupid?"

She turned and looked to see if there was someone else behind her. "Two? Who's number two?"

"Don't play innocent with me."

"Thad, what are you talking about? I haven't done anything."

He straightened from leaning on his car as his expression relaxed. "Oh my goodness, you're telling the truth. So this is all *his* little scheme?"

"Who's *he*?" she nearly screeched. "I don't know who you're talking about!" She was too tired, and she was verging on hysterical, and she really, really hated that feeling. She had to get away from this man.

He came closer to her, and it was all she could do not to shrink back. How had she ever thought she loved his man? She was nearly repulsed right now.

"Hudson Honeywood offered me a job at his practice in exchange for the dog." She didn't think to hide her surprise in time. "That's right. Wow. You really didn't know. I thought you two had cooked up this scheme so you could leave me with the dog. But now I know this is all Hudson's plan to lure you away."

What had Hudson done? She felt sick. She was never going to get Louis away now.

"Don't worry. I'll get you a new puppy." He smiled. "See you at home."

He got into his car and started to back out of his spot before she could move out of the way.

She stepped aside and watched him drive away. What had just happened? She didn't understand. Somehow, she made her way to her car and then sat behind the wheel, trying to think it through, but she didn't know where to start.

Yes, she did. Hudson had done a really stupid thing. She knew he'd done it with good intentions, but that didn't make it any less stupid.

He'd blown her chances with her plan. And what was he thinking—he'd been willing to work with Thad every day for the rest of his life? In a small group practice? Hudson was so lucky that Thad had caught on to his stupid little plan. Otherwise—

Wait.

Thad hadn't said no, had he? She squeezed her eyes shut, trying to recall his exact words. He'd described the deal. He hadn't said that he turned it down.

Her eyes popped open. He wasn't turning it down. He was really going to give up Louis.

Hudson's stupid little plan had *worked*.

But she couldn't let that happen. She couldn't let Hudson do this to himself.

She had to stop this.

She hurried to her car, dove behind the wheel, and stabbed at the dash where her start button had used to be. But this wasn't her car. This was a loaner while hers got fixed. This car needed an actual key. She grabbed her purse and started digging.

Only once she'd backed out of the driveway did she realize what else all this meant: Thad had been willing to give up her dog. He hadn't known that she was going to leave him. And yet he'd given up the dog. He'd chosen his career advancement over her emotional needs. She shook this thought out of her head. What did it matter now?

She reached the ranch in record time, her heart racing as she killed her engine in the driveway. The whole world went silent, and she wished she had Louis with her for support. She looked out the windshield at the cute little ranch house in front of her. What a nice place. So simple. So unpretentious.

Was she really going to do this? Just walk up to some man's door? Some man who wasn't her boyfriend?

And this wasn't just any man. This was Hudson Honeywood, the gorgeous, kind doctor who had gone out of his way to protect her and then kissed her like no man had ever kissed her before.

Tenderly. Sweetly. Meaningfully. She shook her head. This was hard enough without thinking about that kiss. She forced her feet to carry her toward the door as she tried to slow her heart rate.

He opened it before she got there, concern etched on his face. "What's wrong?"

The sight of him made it hard to speak but after an uncomfortable pause, she found the words. "I know what you did."

He chuckled dryly. "That sounds like a line out of some crime drama."

She didn't join him in his laughter. Her chest hurt.

Understanding dawned on his face. "*Oh.*" He sighed and put his hands on his hips. "He told you?" His surprise was evident.

She wished that she could say, "Of course he did." She wished she had the kind of boyfriend who told her things like that, but they both knew that she didn't.

"He didn't have to tell me."

Hudson smiled wryly. "Figures. I should have known you were too smart not to figure it out." He stepped back and swept his arm in invitation. "Would you like to come inside?" She did want to go inside. She was curious what Hudson's house looked like, and she wanted to be inside of it. "Is there anyone else there?"

His arm dropped is if the arm itself were disappointed. "I admire your prudence. No, no one else is home." He pulled the door shut behind him as he stepped out onto the small porch. Suddenly the quarters were too close even though they were out in the open on the South Dakota plains, and she stepped down off the porch. He followed her, but he still stood so close that she could feel the life force coming off his body.

"Hudson, you can't do this. It will ruin your life."

He chuckled. "You are mistaken if you think that guy can ruin anything about my life."

She shook her head. He wasn't getting it. "You don't want someone like him in your office, in the business you've worked so hard to build." He wasn't getting this. How could she make it clear. "Thad doesn't *like* you!"

"I don't care if crazy people don't like me. They're crazy."

While his words made some logical sense, she still didn't see how they could be true. "You might not consciously care, but just being around someone who irritates you is going to make your life less pleasant."

"You know what makes my life less pleasant?" His voice grew stronger with each word. "You being with Drake. *That* makes my life less pleasant. I want to take you out on a real date. I want to sweep you off your feet and then spend the rest of my life loving you and caring for you. I want to start that process right now. If the holdup is a dog custody battle, then it's worth me working with Drake."

His words stole her breath away, and she had no argument. She just stared at him. "I don't think I can let you do this." It was a weak argument, but it was the only one she had.

"While I admire your strength as an independent woman, it's really not up to you to let me or not let me do anything."

Of course, she knew this was true. Why had she said something so foolish? "What if I say I won't go out with you if you do this?"

His eyes grew wide "Are you serious?"

She didn't know if she was serious, but her current hand didn't offer a lot of cards to play.

He waited for her to answer, and when she did, he said, "Well, then I guess I just give you your dog and bid you adieu. It's still worth it to set you free of him."

She took a step back. Was he serious?

He took one big step, erasing the gap she had just created. He took her hand in his. "Evelyn, I've been waiting my whole life for you. Now that you're here, I don't want to wait another second. Life is short. Let's stop wasting it. Who cares what my work life is like if I get to come home to you?"

Tears sprang to her eyes, and she didn't know if they were happy tears, scared tears, or shock tears.

"This deal was his idea, Evelyn. He chose his job. He chose a career opportunity over you, over your feelings, over your need for Louis. I choose you, Evelyn. I will always choose you." He gently took her cheek into his palm, tilted his head, and kissed her again, and somehow it was even sweeter than the first time.

Chapter 31

Hudson broke the kiss because he was feeling too much too fast. He didn't want to rush things, and he didn't want to accidentally push Evelyn.

She looked up at him, and her eyes were wet. He gently wiped a tear from the corner of her eye. She smiled, but her eyes stayed sad.

"What is it?" he whispered.

She shook her head. "I know that you can live with it, but what if I can't?" She sniffed. "Please. I want a clean break. If I'm going to fall in love with you, I want to be able to come visit you at work. I want to be able to ask you how your day was without worrying about what you're going to say about Thad. I don't ever want to think about him again. If he works for you, then he will be like a ghost who haunts me, reminding me of this stupid, embarrassing chapter of my life."

His resolve was weakening. "But what about Louis?"

"I don't know, but we'll find another way. I know that Thad doesn't want him, and I know he won't hurt him."

Hudson wasn't so sure about that.

"I don't have a plan yet." She chuckled through her tears. "I just know that your plan really stinks."

"It wasn't my plan," he reminded her. "It was Thad's."

"Well, no surprise that it stinks then, is there?"

Hudson sighed. "Fine."

Her eyes brightened. "Really?"

"Yes, really. You make a good case."

"Oh, thank you!" She hugged him, pressing the side of her face into his chest. His arms went around her of their own accord, and she squeezed him around the waist.

Her embrace felt perfect. When she loosened it, he was disappointed. "Will you call him? Please?"

"I don't have his personal number."

Her face fell.

Right. *She* had his personal number whether she wanted it anymore or not. "Okay, I'll call him." He held his hand out for the phone. Then he plugged the number into his own cell. He didn't want to further complicate things by letting Drake know that Evelyn was standing right beside him.

"Hey, Drake, so I apologize for this, but I have to change my mind."

He growled into his phone. "What? You gave me your word!"

"I did not. I told you that I would talk to my partner." He looked down at Evelyn's pretty, long eyelashes. He had not specified which partner he would discuss it with. "But you caught me off guard with your request, and now that the dust has settled, I realize that your idea just won't work. But I would still like to adopt the dog if your price still stands." He waited for Drake to answer, and when he didn't, he pulled the phone away from his ear to look at the screen.

Drake had hung up.

Hudson sighed and looked at Evelyn. "We'd better get to brainstorming."

Chapter 32

Evelyn didn't realize that she was starving until Hudson mentioned food. He offered to cook for her, but she didn't think it was appropriate to be alone with him in his house yet. Not that she felt unsafe. Quite the opposite. She had never felt safer than she felt when she was with Hudson. But just in case anyone showed up, she didn't want to be there, since she hadn't officially broken up with Thad yet.

Hudson didn't blink when she declined his offer, which she appreciated. Thad would have been offended, but Hudson just said, "Want to go to the diner in town?"

So that's what they did, and she ordered some unhealthy comfort food. Then, when Hudson ordered a salad, she felt self-conscious and wished she'd let him order first. Then she would have followed his lead. She was hungry enough to choke down a salad. Once the server had walked away, Evelyn asked, "That's all you're going to have?" A big, strapping man like that?

"They serve pretty big salads here."

She had her doubts, but they had bigger problems to solve than Hudson's diet.

"Okay," Hudson said, "I've got to admit that I've already given this dilemma a lot of thought, and the only thing I could think of was to offer to buy the dog, which I've already tried. And I'm ashamed to say that Drake outsmarted me."

She laughed out loud when he told her the amount he'd been willing to pay for Louis. Maybe Hudson wasn't quite the genius she thought he was. "I think we need to come at it from a different angle," she said thoughtfully.

"Obviously," Hudson said. He sounded discouraged. "But what angle?"

"Well, I can tell you that Thad's biggest weakness is his pride."

"I think that's every man's biggest weakness."

His words surprised her. If Hudson had a problem with pride, he was doing a great job of hiding it.

"Any idea how we could exploit that?" he asked.

She put her head in her hands. She felt evil. Even though she was mad at Thad, and even though she knew he didn't care one iota about the dog, she still felt guilty scheming against him. He was no Sampson, but she still felt a little like Delilah. If only it could be as easy as a haircut. This gave her another thought. "Vanity. That's another weakness."

Hudson looked intrigued. "What do you mean by vanity? Does he take a lot of selfies?"

She giggled. "Not that I know of. I just meant that he cares a great deal about how he appears to other people, about what they think of him."

Hudson scowled. "You're kidding. He doesn't behave that way in the hospital."

"Good point. You're right. He doesn't care what you think of him unless he respects you, and he doesn't respect most of the people he encounters."

"Who *does* he respect?" His tone suggested that the answer was no one.

"He respects people who make a lot of money. People who have professions that mean that they're smart. So lawyers, college professors …" She was having trouble coming up with more examples. "Maybe it's a pretty short list."

"Doctors?" Hudson offered.

She nodded. "Definitely other doctors, especially those who are further along in their careers than he is."

"But not nurses," Hudson said.

"Definitely not nurses." Drake had hidden this from her for a long time, but now she knew it to be true.

"So isn't he going to be really embarrassed when a lowly nurse breaks up with him?" He put air quotes around *lowly nurse*.

"Yes, probably." The thought made her sad. He wasn't even going to miss her. He was just going to be annoyed that people knew that she'd left him.

Hudson was staring at her.

"What?"

"That's it."

"What?" She didn't like being left behind.

"You have decided that you're going to break up with him, right?"

She rolled her eyes. "I can understand why you would doubt me, but please, yes."

"Breaking up with him is going to make him look bad to his peers."

She still didn't know where he was going, but she was trying really hard to keep up. She felt like a basset hound chasing a cheetah. "So you want me to offer to keep it quiet?" That couldn't be the whole plan. It wasn't enough.

"Sort of." Hudson chewed his lip.

"Oh, just spill it. Obviously you have a plan."

He shook his head. "I don't have a plan yet, and I've learned that rushing into one isn't a good idea with this guy. But I'm thinking something along the lines of you letting him break up with you."

Her eyes widened as she thought about it. "So what do I say? Please break up with me?"

"You say something like, 'Drake, I will let everyone believe whatever you want them to believe about our breakup. Spin it however you want to spin it. Just give me the dog.'"

"I don't want to lie." The plan wasn't exactly evil, but she still felt icky.

"You won't have to. He'll do all the lying. You just have to ignore whatever he says. And hey …" He reached across the table and took her hand. "It's just an idea. If you don't want him spouting lies about you, I get that."

"What if he says something really horrible?" She could already hear his words. He would accuse her of cheating on him with Hudson and say he kicked her to the curb. Maybe something even worse.

"Like I said, you don't have to do it." His voice was gentle. Soothing.

Evelyn remembered his words from earlier. He didn't care what a crazy person thought of him. Did she? Anyone with any sense knew what Thad was like. If someone chose to believe him, did she really care what that person thought of her? "Okay."

"Okay? You want to try it?"

She nodded. "Let's give it a whirl. After supper. I will talk to him. Make the breakup official and try to make this plan work."

Hudson looked at me. "You want to come up with a plan B while we're here?"

"Isn't *this* the plan B?"

He chuckled. "No, this is plan C. You had a plan A, which I messed up with my hastily devised plan B." She could see the regret in his eyes. "But do you want to come up with a plan D while we're here?"

She shook her head. "I don't want to think about him anymore. We don't need a plan D unless this one doesn't work. Let's just enjoy our supper."

Chapter 33

Chase sat in the top row of the ancient wooden bleachers of the auction house. His long legs were bent at a painful angle, but an elderly woman in front of him was leaning on them, so he didn't want to move. It had happened so gradually that he wasn't even sure she knew she was leaning on them, and he was afraid even the slightest movement would make her aware and embarrass her. So he was working very hard to hold still.

When he had first come home from overseas, Hudson had suggested the local livestock auction as a way for Chase to safely go out in public. "They are your kind of people," Hudson had said. "You won't have to talk to anyone, and you can leave whenever you want to." That was usually the case—when he hadn't become someone's recliner.

Hudson was pretty smart, though Chase didn't love admitting it in front of him. Didn't want to give Hudson a bigger head. He was already the smartest among them. So Chase had started going to the auction for his mental health, but then he'd continued going just in case a horse showed up who needed him.

It had become a part of his routine, and that was another thing that was good for his mental health—routine.

Chase hadn't yet bought a horse at this auction, but he'd been tempted by a few mares over the last several months, and when that happened, he carefully eyed the people placing bids. He knew most of them and could infer their intentions, but if any of the bidders, whether he knew them or not, ever gave him a bad vibe, he would have bid against them.

But mostly he was just waiting for the horse who looked right at him and said, *Bring me home*. So far that hadn't happened, and that was okay. He didn't need another horse just yet. Couldn't even really afford one. But he would be there just in case one needed him.

Today, someone had brought in a whole herd of Nigerian dwarf goats, so there were more people in attendance than usual, some he knew weren't from West Hope. He didn't know everyone in the town, of course, but sometimes he could just tell someone was from away.

There were enough people there to make him uncomfortable but not enough to give him a panic attack. He wished the auction would bring out the goats, but he knew they would save them for last because they knew a lot of people had shown up for them. And while those people waited around for their new pet goats, they might also buy a few scrawny roosters or a few steamed hot dogs. Might as well try to make an extra buck or two.

From the attached barn, he heard a pig squeal. Right. The miniature goats wouldn't be dead last. That honor was always reserved for the swine, but Chase would be long gone before that happened. Their angry, terrified squealing was more than he could take.

The gate opened, and Chase's spine straightened as the young worker led a new horse into the ring. It was a beautiful horse, but that's not what had Chase on alert. Chase could feel the stallion's energy.

The horse was terrified. But underneath that terror ran a strong confident current, and that's what made Chase worry about the young man handling him.

That kid had no idea what he was holding onto. If that horse decided to take charge, the kid would be mincemeat. *Should I jump up and go down there?* Just in case the kid needed a hand? *Yes, I should.* He could go lean on the panels with all the older looky-loos who never sat down for long because it hurt too much. But then everyone would be able to see him. Though he wouldn't be on stage—not even close—he would feel like he was on stage. And what about this woman in front of him?

People started bidding, but not as many as usual. Chase wasn't the only person there who knew this horse was sour. It started stamping, and the bids stopped. The auctioneer kept talking, but his eyes slid sideways to the horse. The kid holding the lead remained complacent.

The ring was small, and the kid tried tugging on the lead to bring the horse around the perimeter, but that stallion didn't want to be led deeper into the hot, stuffy ring in front of the bleachers full of people.

The horse obviously had trust issues.

Chase saw it happening before it happened. The horse didn't want to move. The man tending the gate came toward the horse's rear. Chase wanted to yell, but he knew it wouldn't make any difference. "Sorry, ma'am," he muttered, and he stood. She tipped backward with a small yelp as the man slapped the horse's rear. The startled animal kicked back with a rear leg. The man, who had been smart enough not to stand directly behind the horse, was also smart enough to try to dodge that kick, so it only grazed his side. Still he cried out, but this was mostly drowned out by the stallion's snort, which was followed by the corporate gasp from the audience as the horse reared, pawing at the air. The bewildered teenager let go of the lead, and the horse bolted.

Chase ran down the bleachers and headed for the end of the ring that the horse had just left. The stallion had nowhere to go, and Chase knew he would turn and come back. By the time he did, Chase was pushing off the top of the panel.

His boots hit the dirt inside the ring, and he held his arms out wide as the stallion charged toward him. Chase looked directly into those wide, wild, dark eyes. *I got you*, he said without saying a word. *I got you.*

The horse slowed and banked left before circling around to look at Chase again. Chase exhaled. "Good boy," he whispered. "Very good boy." He approached slowly, with confidence. As soon as he was close enough, he reached out and ran a hand down its neck. "I got you," he said again, aloud this time. He grabbed the lead and slowly turned the horse toward the gate. He looked up at the auctioneer. "What's your highest bid?" he asked. Then he said, "Double it."

The barn workers told him to take the horse immediately. He could pay later. When he explained that he didn't even have a trailer with him, they told him to load the horse into one of theirs. He did so with ease. Once he was tied up, he said, "Let's get you home."

He hurried to go get his truck and back it up to the trailer. Then he went back inside to write a check.

While he was waiting in line, his phone chirped at him. He had an alert set for newly posted basset hounds for sale. Oddly, one had just been posted in West Hope. He clicked on the ad. What on earth? That was Louis! He zoomed in for a closer look. What were the chances? No way Evelyn would sell that dog. So maybe it wasn't Louis. But one glance into those soulful eyes and Chase knew.

It was Louis.

Chase sent a message. When could he come get the dog? Right away. Great, he would be there in thirty minutes. He tucked his phone into his back pocket and stepped up to the auction's office window to pay for his horse.

He was going to be bringing a few new friends home to the ranch tonight. Maybe he would see a stray cat on the way so he could complete the trifecta.

Chapter 34

Hudson reached for the check, and his hand fell on top of Evelyn's. He let it stay there for a moment, enjoying the feeling of her soft skin. "You're kidding right?"

She smiled sheepishly and pulled her hand away. "Thank you."

"You're welcome." He picked up the check and slid out of the booth. He didn't want to leave the diner. He didn't want to let her go see Drake. But sitting in this cozy diner all night wasn't going to get Louis back.

He paid the check, left a big tip, and then followed Evelyn outside. He hurried to open the truck door for her. "I guess we should have brought two vehicles, now that we know the plan involves you driving right back into town."

"It's okay. I'm grateful to have a few more minutes to psych myself up."

He started toward the ranch, and they rode in silence for a few minutes.

"Mind if I turn on some music?" she asked. Before he could answer, she pressed the button, and the cab filled with the sound of classical piano.

He winced, expecting her to make fun of him, but she leaned her head back, closed her eyes, and said, "That's nice. I can almost feel my blood pressure going down."

He smiled as he turned his eyes back to the road. She just kept getting better and better. She wasn't just a pretty nurse who was good to her grandfather. She was a complex, sophisticated, brilliant woman with lots of layers, and he couldn't wait to discover each of them.

But first—they had one small obstacle in their way.

Hudson thought back to the kiss they had shared under the fallen grocery store. He still believed that had been wrong, but what a great mistake to make. It was certainly turning out okay for him. Had he known then, somehow, that she really was the one? Maybe he'd had some inkling that she wouldn't be with Drake much longer.

They reached the ranch, and he walked her to her new car, which wasn't very new. "Are you sure you don't want me to go with you?" He knew she could handle it, but he was feeling so protective that he didn't want to let her out of his sight.

"I'm sure, but thank you."

"I don't have to get out of the car." He glanced at his pickup. "Or the truck."

She smiled sweetly. "I'm sure. I'll call you when it's over?"

He nodded. "Maybe we could even meet up for a few minutes. I've got to run back into town."

She quirked an eyebrow. "Seriously? Wow, we're really ramming the roads today."

He laughed. He'd never heard that expression. "I guess. I've got to get to the farm store. I was going to go after work, but ... well, I got a little distracted. Anyway, Chase used to do the farm store runs, but there's a new woman working there who's a little too flirty, so he refuses to go in there now."

She giggled. "Oh my word. That poor man." She opened her car door and then stopped and looked at him. She took a deep breath. "Here I go."

"Here you go." Every cell in his body wanted to go with her or follow her, but if she wanted to do this alone, then he had to honor that.

"I'll call you soon." She got in and backed out of his driveway without another look at him.

He watched her drive away and then, as he returned to his own truck, he whispered, "God, please let her have that dog," and an odd peace settled over him. This was all going to be okay. All of it, including Louis.

Chapter 35

Evelyn had almost accepted Hudson's offer to go with her to Thad's house. Almost. But she was a big girl. She got herself into this, and she was going to get herself out.

She drove slowly, though, in no hurry to face the music. On her way, she met a pickup pulling a livestock trailer. She didn't recognize Chase until he waved to her. She glanced in the rearview mirror for another look at the trailer. Did that mean he bought a livestock trailer or that he bought some livestock? Either way, good for him.

She turned off her engine and then sat there for a moment longer praying for strength and courage. She had never been scared of Thad, so she didn't know why she was scared now.

Even though she had taken to just walking into his house without knocking, this time she stopped and rapped her knuckles on the door. He took his time answering, which didn't surprise her, and the sardonic look on his face annoyed her enough to defuse some of her fear. She glanced at the floor by his feet expecting to see Louis, but he wasn't there. Out of habit she almost called for him, but she stopped herself. She needed to focus on her task.

"Could we chat for a moment?" She stepped back to let him come outside, but he stepped deeper into the house. Fine. They could do this inside even though she didn't want to. She stepped into his kitchen and shut the door behind her, but she stayed near the door and she kept her jacket on. She scanned the kitchen and what she could see of the living room for Louis. Where was he? He always came running when she came inside, or his version of running, anyway. And if he wasn't snoozing by his food bowl, he would be curled up asleep on the ottoman, but he wasn't in either of those places. Where was he? Fear gnawed at her stomach as she looked at Thad with suspicion. *Focus. Just get through this.* She took a deep breath and spoke, "I don't want to take up much of your time. Obviously, this isn't working. We might already be broken up, I don't know, but I wanted to make it official."

He sneered but didn't say anything.

"And you know that I love Louis. I did not ask Hudson to get involved. He was just trying to help me, but I am willing to buy Louis if you're willing to make the sale."

"Now why would I do that? Why would I want to make things easy for you when you have insulted and humiliated me like this?"

And there it was. She knew him pretty well. And he had no idea how much he was in fact making it easy for her.

"I don't want to humiliate you. In fact, if you let me have Louis, I'll let you tell your side of the story, and I won't tell mine. You can save face with whoever you want, say whatever you want, and I won't argue."

This offer caught him by surprise. She could see his wheels turning, and she shuddered to think of the story he was spinning. Finally, he said, "That's a nice offer. I might have even taken it, but sorry, I already sold the stupid mutt."

She staggered back, forgetting there was a wall there and bumping into it. She was wordless. Breathless. She only stared up at him, at that smug expression. What had he done?

Finally, she managed, "You did what?" Her voice was weak and shaky, and she hated it. Her chest stayed tight with panic. Where was he? Was she never going to see him again? How was she going to know he was okay? "Who did you sell him to?" Maybe she could go buy him back.

Thad shrugged dramatically. "Didn't ask the guy's name. Don't worry," he said patronizingly, "he seemed nice enough, though he didn't pay nearly as much as Hudson was offering." He gave her a sinister smile, and she felt ill. How could she have been so wrong about him? She'd known he wasn't perfect, of course, but she had never suspected he could be this cruel.

"Why would you do this to me?" She'd been so good to him.

"Why would you humiliate me by cheating on me with Honeywood?"

"I didn't cheat—" She stopped herself. She didn't need to defend herself to this guy, and it wouldn't do any good anyway. "Please, Thad, tell me who you sold him to, and I'll still let you tell people whatever you want about us. You can say you broke up with me. You can say I cheated on you. You can tell them I'm a monster and that you're a saint. Just tell me who you sold him to."

"I wish I could, but I didn't ask the guy's name."

"What was his number then?" She could call him and make him an offer.

"Sorry, I deleted it." He was lying. Her eyes scanned the room for his phone. Why, she didn't know. It wasn't like she'd be able to wrestle it away from him.

"Goodbye, Evelyn." He opened the door and stepped toward her, crowding her out of his house.

"Was he from West Hope?"

He shook his head. "I don't think so. He had a weird accent." He kept moving, forcing her to back out of his house. "By the way, I'll be telling my side of the story anyway. You say whatever you want. Who do you think they'll believe?"

The door slammed shut. She stood there for a second, frozen. Then she turned and tried to keep her chin up as she walked, but her legs shook all the way to the car. Absurdly, she scanned Thad's small yard for signs of Louis. She couldn't help it, even though she knew it made no sense. She was too desperate for common sense or logic. Obviously, Louis hadn't escaped his new owner and come running back to her. Obviously, he wasn't hiding behind some bush, but she kept looking.

Maybe she'd be looking for him for the rest of her life. Behind every bush. In every yard she drove by. The tears came then, and she sat behind the wheel sobbing. She had to get out of this driveway.

She had to get away from this house, but she didn't know if it was safe to drive.

She decided she would just drive to the nearest gas station and then sit there until she could get a grip.

She pulled into the first station she saw; seconds later Hudson pulled in beside her. She'd never been so happy to see him, and she jumped out of the car, flung her arms around him, and buried her wet face in his chest. His body stiffened, and she thought he was irritated, so she pulled back a little. But when she looked up at his face she saw that it was clouded with anger.

"What happened?" he asked, his voice a low growl.

"He sold Louis." She couldn't bring her herself to say more. She nuzzled into him again. She didn't know what else to do. The grief and fear were overwhelming.

"Sold him to who?"

She shook her head without looking up. "He said he didn't know him. He posted online, and someone came and took him. Thad said he was from away, that he had an accent. He wouldn't give me the guy's number."

Hudson's body tightened again, but he held her there for several minutes, letting her cry, before saying, "Look, I know it's getting late, but I don't want to leave you alone like this. Why don't you come back to the ranch for a bit? Chase will be there, and on most nights, at least one other brother will be too. They can't seem to stay away." He lifted her chin and looked at her. "Can I drive you back there? I'll bring you back to your car whenever you're ready."

She nodded. She didn't know what else to do.

Chapter 36

Hudson felt sick. What had he done? Why had he gotten in the middle of this? He had to fix it. He would ask Drake who he'd sold the dog to. He would *make* Drake tell him. He didn't know how yet, but he would do it.

He would find out who had Louis, and then he would buy him back. No way that buyer had paid Thad as much as Hudson was willing to pay. He could fix this.

But first, he needed to get Evelyn to the ranch. Chase would be home from the auction by now. He could stay with her while Hudson went back into town to sort this out.

Ramming the roads indeed.

He kept sneaking glances at her, and it hurt to look at her. He could feel her heart breaking.

What an awful human being Thad Drake was. Hudson really tried to see the good in people, and usually could, but this guy? Nah. Nothing good to see.

He pulled into his driveway and saw a livestock trailer backed up to the garage. Whoa. Had Chase actually bought something at the auction? This might not work then. Chase might not be willing to hang out with Evelyn if he had a horse to tend to. Oh well, Evelyn could hang out in the barn. It was still better than a gas station parking lot.

Hudson hoped his little trip to Drake's house wouldn't take long, anyway.

He killed the engine and heard something that surprised him.

Barking.

He looked at Evelyn, who had stopped sniffling and was staring out the windshield with wide eyes. "Am I losing it, or ..." She didn't finish the sentence.

"Chase has been wanting to get a dog ever since—"

"That's not just any dog." She flung the truck door open.

"Wait!" Hudson leapt out to go after her. Was there a chance Chase was the buyer? Sure. But it wasn't a very good chance, and he didn't want Evelyn to get her hopes up to be crushed again. But she was running to the barn like a kid to a giant gumball machine. "Be careful!" he yelled. It was dark, and he didn't want her to roll her bad ankle.

He didn't know whether she heard him, but she didn't slow down.

Chapter 37

Evelyn would know that baying bark anywhere. The barn was lit up, but all else was dark, and her eyes searched the property for her best friend.

And then she saw him, running toward her, his ears flopping up and down like the wings of an albatross. He kept barking as he came, the barn light shining behind him to make him look all the more like a miracle.

She fell to her knees as they met, and he pummeled his tunnel-shaped body into hers. She caught him and fell sideways to the grass, keeping her arms around him. He wiggled in her embrace, but he didn't try to escape, and he stopped barking.

"Wow," Hudson said from behind her. "It's really him?"

Only a little embarrassed at what this amazing man had just witnessed, she said, "Yeah. It's him."

"I'm sorry. I shouldn't have doubted. What happened?"

At first, she thought he was asking her and didn't know what to say. What had happened? She had no idea! She'd been with Hudson! How was she supposed to have solved his mystery in the last thirty seconds? But then she heard another man's voice and knew Hudson hadn't been talking to her.

"I saw the ad online and recognized him, so I went and got him."

She got herself together enough to sit on her butt, criss-cross-applesauce, and look up to see it was Chase speaking. Louis lay beside her, panting. His hundred-yard dash had really tuckered him out.

"So he's really yours?" she said, not quite daring to hope. "That's it? He sold him to you?"

"No, he's really *yours*," Chase said, "as he has been since the day he met you. And yes, I paid for him, but not much, and don't worry about that."

Evelyn didn't think she'd ever been so happy. "Wow, you two Honeywoods make quite the heroic pair."

"Uh, but you're going to choose me, right?" Hudson said. He actually sounded nervous, which was adorable.

Chase grunted and headed back to the barn.

"Did you buy a horse?" Hudson called after him.

Chase lifted one hand into the air. "I bought a horse!" He did not turn around or stop walking.

Hudson helped her to a stand, and she didn't take her eyes off Louis. "Don't worry, he's not ever going to leave your side now."

"Good thing."

Hudson bent down to pet him. "Good boy, Louis. You did a good job finding your mama." He straightened and looked at her. "Let me give you two a ride home? Or back to your car? Whichever you want."

She nodded. "Thank you." Tears slid down her cheeks, but she was too tired to deal with them. The exhaustion had come on suddenly, and it was overpowering.

"You're welcome."

Slowly they went to the car, and she tried to hide the fact that her ankle ached. She'd thought it was all healed up, but she probably shouldn't have been sprinting across a field in the dark in Danskos.

He opened the truck for her, and she bent down to give Louis a boost.

Hudson laughed at this, and she let him. It was pretty funny. She would now be Louis's servant for the rest of his life.

Hudson caught her arm before she climbed into the truck. And then before she knew what was happening, his lips were on hers. She kissed him back, and their arms went around each other, making her whole body warm.

Hudson pulled away, but he didn't let go. "Be my girlfriend."

She nodded. "Okay, but I don't want to call you my boyfriend."

"What?" His alarm was evident.

"You're not a boy. You're very much a man."

"Okay, call me whatever you want as long as you call me yours."

"Oh, smooth talker," she tried to say, but he interrupted her with another kiss.

This time, when he pulled back, he said, "I am madly in love with you, Evelyn Cotton. I think I've loved you since the first time

I saw you. Maybe even since the first time I heard your voice on the phone."

She giggled. That wasn't possible, but it sure was romantic. "I don't know when I started loving you, Hudson, but it might have been when you got me that big bag of cheese."

He laughed heartily. "Did you just say you love me?"

"Yeah. I think that's what I said."

He leaned forward to lay his forehead against hers. "I hope this is the beginning of forever, and you know what else I hope?"

She had no idea. "No, what?"

"I hope that I don't spend the rest of our life together wondering if you love me as much as you love that dog."

She laughed. "I have enough love to go around."

He narrowed his eyes. "Okay, I guess that's good enough for now." He helped her into the truck. Louis was already sitting in the middle of the bench seat, tall and proud, looking out the windshield, ready for adventure.

Hudson got behind the wheel and gave Louis a wry look. "I'm not sure how much I like you being between us there, bud."

Evelyn had already buckled up, but now she unbuckled and slid Louis up and over her lap as she moved to the middle.

"There. That's better," Hudson said as her new seatbelt clicked into place. She looped her arm through his and sighed. She'd never been so happy. She'd never felt so safe.

Hudson started the engine. "Let's get you two home." And then he sneezed.

"God bless you," Evelyn said as a reflex.

"Thank you. Yes, God has certainly blessed me."

Epilogue

They had rehearsed this. More than once. And when they had rehearsed it, Louis had acted bored, lying down with his chin resting on his paws, his eyes droopy and sad because his mother was ignoring him.

Oh, but not now. Not now that it mattered. Not now that the barn was filled with loved ones waiting expectantly for the blushing bride to appear.

Now, Louis was barking his head off. Evelyn could imagine the look on Hudson's face. Could imagine his efforts to get Louis to shush. Over the last months, the two had bonded quite a bit. They had formed a real friendship, but apparently Louis was not listening to his good friend now.

"Maybe we should go in early," Evelyn's childhood friend, her maid of honor, said nervously.

Laurel Bannon, who was the next bridesmaid in line looked over her shoulder. "He just feels Evelyn's nervous energy. He's fine. Don't worry about it, Evelyn."

It was sweet of Laurel to say, but Evelyn didn't have any nervous energy. She'd never been so sure of anything in her life.

Olivia came bustling toward them. "Are you ready?" She whispered even though she didn't need to whisper because they were outside and even the people sitting in the back of the barn wouldn't be able to hear them over the music and Louis howling.

Evelyn nodded. "I am more than ready." She could not wait to be married to this man, to be his wife, to have him for her husband. She could not wait to be a Honeywood. Olivia was one of the few people who understood that enthusiasm. "How's it going in there so far?" Evelyn asked.

"Everything has been perfect. I can't wait for you to see the video of Louis walking down the aisle. He stepped into the barn and then started backing up like he'd changed his mind." Olivia giggled. "Having been a runaway bride myself once, I could commiserate. Anyway, I thought I was going to have to hook a leash to him but then Hudson called to him, and Louis started slinking down the aisle looking over each shoulder as he went. I've never seen anything move so slowly. So suspiciously. And then when he was about halfway down the aisle, he broke into a dead sprint. The little cushion started bouncing up and down on his back, and I was afraid the rings were going to fly off."

"But they didn't?"

Olivia shook her head. "They did not. The dog and rings arrived safely on the stage. It was magical."

Evelyn had been so busy talking to Olivia, she hadn't realized that all the bridesmaids had gone.

It was her turn. Finally, she was about to walk down the aisle. She stepped closer to the door and waited for the music to change. And when it did, she stepped inside blinking as her eyes adjusted to the dimmer lighting. The place was gorgeous. Olivia had done a great job decorating, and the wedding party looked fabulous up front—

Her eyes found Hudson, and she gasped.

Though she loved how he looked in his glasses, he had insisted on wearing his contacts today so that he'd look better for the wedding pictures. She thought this was silly, but now that she was staring at him in his tuxedo, she knew he wasn't wrong.

He took her breath away.

Her eyes fell to Louis, who had finally fallen silent. He sat there looking at her expectantly, right beside Hudson's left leg. The cushion, though askew, was still tied to his back, and she knew him well enough to know that he really hated that. But his cute little purple bow tie, also askew, was what really stole the show. It was the same color as the flowers in the bouquet she carried, which were the same color as the pocket square in Hudson's jacket.

It all matched perfectly. It had all been orchestrated perfectly. This was her family. She was home.

www.ingramcontent.com/pod-product-compliance
Lightning Source LLC
Chambersburg PA
CBHW032217070925
32253CB00016B/164